NAVIGATING NIGHTMARES

HARE-RAISING SUMMER

BY A.C. BAUER

CAT EYE PRESS

Hare-Raising Summer by A.C. Bauer
Copyright © 2026 A.C. Bauer

No part of this publication may be reproduced, distributed, or transmitted in any form or by any means, including photocopying, recording, or other electronic or mechanical methods, without the prior written permission of the publisher, except for the use of brief quotations in a book review. Additionally, no part of this book may be used or reproduced in any manner for the purpose of training artificial intelligence technologies or systems.

The story, all names, characters, and incidents portrayed in this production are fictitious. No identification with actual persons (living or deceased), places, buildings, and products is intended or should be inferred.

Book Cover Design by Brian Remillard

ISBN (Paperback): 979-8-9913367-4-1
ISBN (Epub): 979-8-9913367-5-8

Published by Cat Eye Press
Cateyepress.com

WARNING!

Do not read this book front to back like you would most other books. Instead, you will need to follow the instructions at the bottom of each page to continue the story. You will be asked from time to time to choose where the story goes, but beware! The choices you make have consequences and can lead you on radically different paths. Are you ready to begin? Turn to **page 1**.

PAGE 1

You pull your suitcase out of the back of the taxi. As soon as the trunk closes with its all too familiar thunk, the taxi pulls away, splattering your jeans with small flakes of wet mud. Before you know it, the taxi hooks a corner, and it's gone. Leaving you all alone.

You turn toward the house.

Well, not all alone. You're staying with your grandparents for the summer while your parents are out living it up on some beachfront vacation rental. At first, you were so excited when they told you the news about the vacation. Then came those three terrible words: no kids allowed. So, you got shipped off here. To "Bunny Buddies Estates," as your grandma calls it.

You pull at your shirt's collar. In the muggy summer heat, it feels tight around your neck, like a python slowly squeezing the life out of its prey.

"Better get this over with," you say and head toward the house.

*Turn to **page 2***

PAGE 2

It's a white, two-story house with a cellar accessible from the outside. Nothing really to write home about. Unless you're obsessed with rabbits.

As you approach the house, you get a whiff of the rabbits out back. Your grandparents have been raising the little furballs for years. They sell them as pets and to other breeders. They also occasionally enter them into contests and fairs. As far as you know, they don't ever eat the things, but you wouldn't be surprised if some of their buyers did. Yuck!

At the front door, you knock three times and let yourself in. You know your grandma never locks up the place. "We're out in the country," she says. "We're far enough away from any trouble worth locking the doors over." Plus, they're expecting you anyway.

You step through the doorway and gasp.

*Turn to **page 3***

PAGE 3

Your grandparents' rabbit collection has exploded since the last time you were here. The little foyer is lined with rabbit knickknacks in every shape, size, and color imaginable. Some lay two or three bunnies deep, haphazardly piled on top of one another. Even the walls are filled with rabbit photos and old-timey illustrations.

Your throat tightens, but you're not sure if it's from the summer heat or the house's musty, rabbit-tinged air. You pull at your collar again. You need something to drink and fast.

You remember where the kitchen is. Surely there's some water in there.

You poke your head out of the foyer and into the rest of the house.

You really should wait for your grandparents to greet you, right? It is their house after all, and that would be the polite thing to do.

But then again, they should know you're coming, and you *are* really thirsty. What's the harm in getting some water while you wait?

What do you do?

Wait patiently by the door on **page 77**

Go the kitchen and get something to drink ASAP on **page 44**

PAGE 4

A chill runs down your spine. "Survive?"

"Yeah," the Rabbit Man says. "They have us playing this fucked-up game. Survive-or-die kind of shit. They're hunting us for some kind of sport. They have this whole place roped off. Try to get too far out, and there's fucking booby traps. I've been running around, trying to find people, pool our resources, you know?"

He grabs the rabbit's foot around his neck, clutches it tightly.

"What's that for?" you ask.

"A rabbit's foot. Worth one point a piece in the game. Whoever has the most by daybreak wins."

"Wins what exactly?"

The Rabbit Man goes quiet for a moment. "Let's not talk about that right now. C'mon, let's get somewhere safe. I know a place."

He slips his hand around your arm and tugs. You pull away from him.

"We need to go. Are you coming or not, kid?"

Is this Rabbit Man really telling the truth? Is there some kind of sick game going on in the woods behind your grandparents' house? Can you really trust this guy?

---

*Go with the Rabbit Man and venture to **page 34***

*Carve your own path on **page 41***

You throw the covers over your face and slide down into your bed. Why did you have to be so fucking nosey? Especially after your grandmother told you not to go into Mr. Bundinni's room. Why?

Your pounding heartbeat almost drowns out the sound of Mr. Bundinni walking toward you, but it's there. Getting louder with each step. The floorboards squeak and squirm under Mr. Bundinni's powerful presence.

You expect to be ripped to shreds any second. Your heart is beating so fast, too fast. So, when you hear a loud boom, you initially think it's your heart exploding. But it's not.

It's the door to your bedroom slamming against the wall. You sit up in bed, the covers falling from your face. You see a shadow by the door. You hear the loading of a shotgun, see the flash, and hear the explosion of an erupting round.

Everything is happening so fast. So slow. Mr. Bundinni screams. Blood splashes across your face and bedsheets. Mr. Bundinni is there one moment, and the next, he's crashing through the bedroom window and tumbling outside.

*Go to **page 48***

PAGE 6

You're in some kind of dimly lit courtroom. To your right are your grandparents. Next to them is a smug-looking Mr. Bundinni. Two officers are on your left. And in front of you, presiding over the gathering, is a man wearing a black hood.

"Grandma! Grandpa! Get me out of here!" you yell.

"SILENCE!" the hooded judge commands with the slam of his gavel.

You look over at your grandparents, but they don't dare look at you. Their focus is squarely on the judge.

"I've dealt with many children in my career," the judge begins, "but never under these particular… circumstances. I've been briefed on tonight's happenings, and I'm appalled…"

Hope spreads across your face. Maybe you're not in trouble after all! Maybe the judge is here to punish Mr. Bundinni instead!

"For a child to witness our most cherished rituals…" the judge begins again. With his words, all hope disappears. "It's irresponsible. But *that* matter shall be dealt with later. Now is the time to decide what to do with the child. So, let me ask you: do you want to do this the hard way or the easy way?"

Hard way. Bring it on. Go to **page 21**

Easy way, please and thank you. Go to **page 42**

Stay silent. Go to **page 85**

You decide to listen to your stomach. You throw off your sheets, creep to the door, and head out into the hallway. A quick look around and you see the hall is dark. Everyone must already be in bed.

You sneak down the stairs and head straight for the kitchen before your stomach can let out another rumble.

In the kitchen, you peel open the heavy fridge door. Unfortunately, the fridge is pretty empty. On the shelves you find a big pitcher of your grandmother's signature nitro lemonade, more celery, a few carrots, and an open box of baking soda. Not your idea of a midnight snack.

You pull open one of the bottom drawers. Score! You find a plastic container of lunch meat!

You crack the lid and are immediately assaulted by the worst scent you've ever smelled. It's not hard to see why. The lunch meat is green and fuzzy. You drop the container back into the fridge and close the door.

Guess you will go to bed hungry after all.

You turn to head back upstairs when something catches your eye. Through the kitchen window, you see two figures walking in the backyard. A closer look out the window and you realize it's your grandma and grandpa.

Turn to **page 80**

PAGE 8

The truth comes pouring out of you faster than lemonade out of a tipped-over cup. You end your spiel with a plea: "You've got to get me out of here!"

The rabbits take a moment to process what you've said. They look at each other.

And then they break out laughing.

You're on your own, kiddo.

*Go to **page 93***

PAGE 9

That night, you're lying in bed. You still don't know if you should tell your grandpa about Smalls or just let it be. It's just one rabbit after all.

Yeah, maybe it's not that big of a deal. Rabbits get loose all the time, right? Look what happened on your first day here. A wave of relief washes over you. Maybe now you'll finally get some sleep.

After you get some water, that is.

You climb out of bed and head toward the kitchen. As you near the kitchen, you hear something. A dripping sound. But also, a wet lapping sound; the kind of sound you'd expect a thirsty dog to make.

You creep toward the kitchen. A wedge of light from the refrigerator illuminates the room. You stop at the doorway and cannot believe your eyes.

*Seeing is believing on **page 144***

PAGE 10

You decide it's probably best to do what the Hare wants and take him to your grandparents' house.

It takes you a little bit, but you manage to find your way back to the path you came in on. You and the Hare come to the edge of the tree line. You see your grandparents' house emerge through the thicket of trees.

As soon as you exit the woods and enter the backyard, the Hare grabs you by the arm. His grip is firm and tight, squeezing you like a malfunctioning blood pressure cuff.

"Hey!" he shouts into the night. "Think I got something that belongs to you!"

There's a long period of silence. And then the shed door opens, and your grandparents emerge. As they walk toward you, the Hare places the dead cop's gun next to your temple.

"L-l-let the kid go," your grandpa says. His voice is shaky. Uncertain and unconfident.

"Not until I get what I want," the Hare spits back. He nuzzles the gun harder into the side of your head.

"Anything! Just let the kid go," your grandma pleads.

She lurches forward, reaching out for you. In a flash, the gun is pointed away from you and toward—

BAM!

*Turn to **page 83***

It's just too much of a risk. You don't want your grandparents getting hurt. Or worse.

You spend the next few days making lemonade under constant supervision. Even your nap and bathroom breaks are supervised.

Your life descends into a bizarre routine of sleep and lemonade-making. Meanwhile, the monster rabbits' numbers grow and multiply. Exactly like you'd expect with rabbits. You know Bunny Buddies Estates has a lot of rabbits, but you suspect that Smalls is bringing in wild rabbits too. Either way, it becomes impossible to escape. There are just too many of them.

Your suspicions are confirmed when the guards start bringing in people you've never seen before to make the lemonade alongside you.

The reign of the telepathic monster bunnies has just begun, and you know it's all over for humanity.

PAGE 12

You tell the cop everything. About Mr. Bundinni. Your grandparents. The shrine in the shed. Your eyes blur with tears when you talk about the death of the rabbit and the blood-drinking.

After you're done, you expect the cop to say something. Something comforting or perhaps launch into a line of questioning. Instead, he's as silent as can be. He keeps his focus on the road ahead. You wipe the tears from your eyes and wait.

Eventually, the car slows to a stop. You look over at the cop, but he doesn't meet your gaze. You turn to look out the window. Your eyes go wide when you realize where you are.

Turn to **page 59**

You have no choice.

You picture the outcome in your head, over and over. You close your eyes, shutting off all other stimuli. And yet, one invades your thoughts.

Smalls's voice.

"No… no," he says curtly.

A second passes and your thoughts intensify. His voice grows louder in your head.

"No! No! No, no, no, no!"

Your head swims in the thickness of your imagination.

Smalls lets out one last bloodcurdling scream, "NOOOOOOOOO—!"

POP!

The sound explodes in your ears. The mental image is gone. You open your eyes to see that it's become reality.

All that remains of Smalls is a blast zone of thick, red gore scattered across the green grass.

You fall to your knees. Your grandpa and grandma hold you up.

"You did good, kiddo. You did good."

Go to **page 111**

PAGE 14

You spill your guts. You tell her everything. About Mr. Bundinni. The altar. The rabbits. The blood-drinking. All of it. It comes pouring out of you.

By the end you expect her to look at you like you're crazy, but she only nods. A soft smile flashes across her face, and then she says, "I'll be right back."

She disappears around a corner. For every second she's gone, a million thoughts race through your head. What if you are crazy? What if the whole thing was a bad dream or a hallucination? What if—

No. You know what you saw, and you can prove it. One look in that shed and—

The woman returns. She smiles at you, takes your hands in hers, and looks at you like your mother used to.

And then she wraps a pair of handcuffs around your wrists.

Turn to **page 68**

PAGE 15

There's no way you're going to listen to some mysterious voice in the woods. You head to the right.

The path immediately becomes harder to traverse. Sharp, pointy rocks tear your feet open. Your steps become wobbly and uneven. You roll your ankle and fall to the ground.

As you're nursing your injured ankle, a form approaches.

It reaches down and grabs your wrist.

"Now you're coming with me."

*Turn to **page 178***

PAGE 16

You and your grandpa spend the next few hours helping your grandma make batch after batch of lemonade. You're watched the entire time by one of the rabbits who brought you up from the cellar.

After you complete a few batches, one of the monster rabbits usually brings in a normal rabbit and allows it to drink some of the lemonade. Once it's done, the rabbit is brought back outside.

You mull over what to do. You think back to what you told your grandpa in the cellar. Maybe it really is in the dose. Maybe you just need to drink as much lemonade as possible in order for the powers to kick in. But… what if it doesn't work? What if it only works on rabbits? Is that a risk worth taking?

Better decide quick, one way or another.

If you decide to kick off your plan, go to **page 170**

If you decide to play it safe and keep making lemonade, go to **page 11**

Someone screams, and the room fills with a blinding light. You close your eyes, praying everything is okay when you open them.

But it's not.

Your grandmother is gone. The spot where she once stood is empty, except for a pile of ashes.

You fall to your knees and rake your hands through the warm ashes.

"Grandma…?" you squeak.

A second after your heart breaks, pure anger pours out of you.

"What have you done with her?" you roar at Mr. Bundinni.

He smiles and steps toward you. He leans down, looks you right in the eyes, and says, "Do you really want to find out?"

*Tell him yes by going to **page 43***

*Say no by going to **page 62***

PAGE 18

You watch as Smalls continues to grow and grow and grow.

He screams in pain as the cage wraps around him. Blood oozes from where metal meets flesh. Smalls struggles. The cage bulges outward, overflowing with rabbit, but still manages to hold its form.

You look anxiously toward the house.

WHERE ARE YOUR GRANDPARENTS?! WHY AREN'T THEY OUT HERE??

You turn back toward Smalls just as you hear a pop. Like a balloon exploding. But it's not air that's being released.

It's gore.

A shower of red remains rushes out through the ribs of the cage. Splatters all over you, the ground, even the nearby rabbits.

As Smalls drips off you, you know you're in for a bummer summer once your grandpa finds out.

By some miracle, you're able to grab onto the ledge of the pit you were falling into. A wet gurgle from below tells you the cop wasn't so lucky.

You look down to see the cop impaled on a bed of wooden spikes, his blood rushing from the large puncture holes. His body twitches, some semblance of consciousness flickering in his eyes.

It's only then that you realize how close you came to sharing the same fate. Your feet barely dangle above one of the taller spikes.

Oh man. You've got to get out of there and fast.

You quickly turn your attention back to the top of the pit. Your arms are already feeling the strain of your weight. But the ground is feeling loose in your hands.

Pull yourself up and NOW!

---

*If it's been more than a week since you did arm day at the gym, go to **page 156***

*If you've done arm day this week, go to **page 119***

When you wake up in the morning, the campfire is out. Your grandmother is already up and about, packing things into Bertha's saddle pockets.

"Grandma, are we going somewhere?"

"Yeah, kiddo," she says. "I suppose we are. C'mon."

She pulls you off the ground and helps you onto Bertha's back. Without another word, she hops on, and off the two of you go.

The ride is bumpy, but that's what you'd expect from riding on a giant rabbit. The landscape changes in small waves, from strange-looking forests to plains and finally rolling hills.

Somewhere along the way, you get the courage to ask the question that's been on your mind all day. "Where are we going?"

"Well, with you here now, I think I can finally do the one thing I've been meaning to do all these years."

"And what's that?"

"To kill a rabbit god, kiddo."

You reflexively gulp. You cling tighter to your grandmother and hope this isn't just the start of the end.

PAGE 21

You glare at the judge.

"I'm not afraid of you," you say. "I know what I saw. They should be the ones on trial here, not me." You nod toward your grandparents and Mr. Bundinni.

"I thought you might say something like that," the judge says.

He lifts his gavel and slams it down. The bang echoes through the room. All is quiet as the judge announces the verdict.

"Death… by the pit."

*Go to **page 92***

PAGE 22

There's no way you're staying here. You break into a run. The world blurs around you as you head for the road in front of your grandparents' house. Once you've reached the road, you start to run alongside it. You're careful to stay in the grass, so you don't tear up your bare feet on the rocky dirt road.

A few minutes later and you're already out of breath. You slow down, not that it matters much. You're quite a ways away from your grandparents' house. Plus, it's not like you're actually being chased. No one even knows you're out here.

That is, until a red and blue light flashes behind you.

You turn around, blinded by the lights. You hear what sounds like a car door open and then close.

"Now, what's a kid like you doing out in the middle of the night?" There's a bit of a southern drawl to the voice, which isn't that uncommon around here. But there's something else too. An arrogance. A *dangerous* sense of arrogance.

You stay silent. The cop steps away from the patrol car. His heavy boots crunch against the gravel road as he moves toward you.

"Think it might be a good idea for you to come with me," he says. He grabs hold of your shoulder and squeezes.

*Go to **page 78***

"Okay, I'll help."

"Good." He drops you to the ground. "Now, c'mon. We've got work to do."

The two of you return to the house and to the kitchen. The floorboards creak under Smalls's considerable weight. Still, it doesn't seem your grandparents have noticed from their bedroom upstairs.

Smalls barks a single order: "Find the recipe. Now."

You begin to scour the cabinets looking for a cookbook, a recipe box, anything that might have the secret of Grandma's nitro lemonade in it. Minutes pass and you can tell Smalls is getting impatient. He's pacing the room, clutching his swollen head. You can hear him muttering to himself, but you can't make out the words.

When you finally clear the last cabinet with no results, you look at Smalls. His attention immediately snaps to you.

"I-I c-c-can't find it," you squeeze out.

He stares at you for a long moment, the anger growing in his eyes. Suddenly, he tears a cabinet door off its hinges and throws it across the room. It shatters against the wall. Smalls roars and begins raking everything out of the cabinet, sending bowls and plates shattering to the floor below.

You dive under the kitchen table. Wrap your hands around your head for protection, but it's useless. Smalls flips the table and throws it aside. He looms over you.

You know he can read thoughts, so you repeat to yourself *please don't kill me, please don't kill me, please don't kill me.*

Turn to **page 91**

PAGE 24

You sleep in fitful bursts. You keep dozing in and out, in and out. A thin screen of surreal dreams keeps playing in your mind, but you can't seem to wake up. Not fully.

You feel hot and uncomfortable against the scratchy, old comforter. Your hand aches. Burns. Itches. The rest of your body soon follows suit. What is happening? Why won't you just wake up?

You let out a groan of pain and cling to it, hoping it will pull you out of sleep.

Slowly, your strange dream-visions slip away. You're back in your room. It looks bigger now for some reason. Your hand no longer hurts, but you're still rather warm. Like you're wearing a thick coat.

You hop off the bed and land with a soft thump. It's then that you realize why the room looks so big.

*Go to **page 50***

Got to hand it to ya, kiddo. You're persistent. So, here's what happens next.

You head back into the house and crawl into bed. You quickly fall asleep because obviously there's nothing to worry about.

Over the course of the next few days, you help out around the house because that's what a good grandchild would do. And the chores are perfectly normal chores. They're things like painting pentagrams in rabbit blood out in the shed and sticking severed rabbit heads on spikes surrounding the shed.

It's also totally normal that your grandparents take you to the shed in the middle of the night. There's a swirling portal to a hellish rabbit-infested wasteland there, and you're happy to go through it, happy to become a sacrifice to your grandparents' rabbit god, Grandifal. Because what grandchild wouldn't do this for their grandparents? These are perfectly normal things, after all.

The last sounds you hear before you cross through the portal are your grandparents' cheers. Of course, you're too unaware to realize they're not cheers for you, but for the carnivorous rabbits waiting to devour your flesh. As you're ripped to shreds, you die believing that you made your grandparents happy.

THE END

PAGE 26

You point to the right. The cop shoves you forward. Apparently, you'll be taking the lead.

You and the cop follow the path for what feels like forever, but maybe that's just what being with a cop feels like. The path winds through sparse areas of the woods and even some occasional clearings. You wonder if the clearings were made for the game or if they're natural. But something quickly pulls you out of your thoughts.

The cop's hand is on your shoulder. "Hold up," he says. "You hear that?"

A booming, crunching sound. Again and again, it's the sound of twigs breaking, but something else too. Like a heavy stack of books falling to the ground over and over again.

You look around, trying to figure out where the sound is coming from. Whatever it is, it's getting closer. Your heart booms in time with the approaching noise.

Suddenly, you see a massive black form emerge from the darkness of the woods. At first you think it's running toward you, but something about its movement isn't right. It's too quick. Too tall.

Then it clicks.

It's *jumping* toward you.

Jump yourself to **page 69**

You two get closer and closer to Ol' Gonzo. Then in a flash, the rabbit takes off. Your grandpa dives for it, grabs it. The animal squirms like crazy, but your grandpa knows how to wrangle it. He tucks it into the crook of his arm and gets up off the ground.

"You almost got away, little guy," he says. "Better luck next time."

Your grandpa takes the rabbit and places it back in its cage. You help catch the remaining rabbits in much the same way as Ol' Gonzo. Except for the last one.

It's a scrawny little brown rabbit, sitting in the middle of the concrete. Surrounded by bits of broken glass, it appears unbothered. It's lapping up your spilled lemonade. It's so busy drinking the stuff, it doesn't even try to run as your grandpa comes up behind it and snatches it off the ground. It barely puts up a fight as it's put back in its own cage.

"Why is that one all alone?" you ask.

"That's Smalls," your grandpa says. "He's a tiny thing, and I've been trying to feed him a little extra to beef him up. Don't want the other rabbits stealing his food, ya know? Anyway, thanks for the help, kiddo. Couldn't have done it without ya." He gives you a quick shoulder hug and starts to lead you back inside.

You toss a glance back at the puddle of lemonade and broken glass.

"What about the glass?"

"Oh, I'll get it later. Now, let's go inside and get some more lemonade. It's hotter than hell out here."

Relax and have some lemonade on **page 108**

PAGE 28

"I'd like you to meet Mr. Robert Bundinni," your grandma says as a man enters the foyer.

Mr. Bundinni is tall, thin, and incredibly pale. He has a thick shock of white hair on his head. His cheeks are covered in patches of wispy, white hair. His nose is small and pink, like he's recently had a cold or something. He's dressed head-to-toe in a black suit that looks two sizes too small for him.

He reaches out for a handshake, and the suit sleeve pulls back past his wrist. He flashes you a smile with his big, yellow teeth.

You take his hand, shake it, and notice just how big his hands are. You quickly let go and slyly wipe your hand on your pants. You're not sure why exactly you did that, but you just had to get "him" off your hand.

"Nice to meet you, *kiddo*," Mr. Bundinni says. Your grandparents have always called you that, but it sounds sinister coming out of his mouth.

You don't say anything to him and instead turn to your grandma. "Is he a friend of yours or something?"

"Something like that," she says with a smile. She grabs the suitcase out of your hands. "Now, c'mon. Let's get you settled."

*Go to **page 149***

PAGE 29

Mr. Bundinni's room glows from the wavering light of three dozen candles scattered across the room. Black stains cover the walls, and deep scratches mar the floorboards. Even through the small crack in the doorway, you can smell the scent of copper and rotting meat.

You push the door open a little more, and that's when you spot him.

Mr. Bundinni. He's sitting on the floor with his back to the door. Rocking back and forth, muttering to himself. Sweat gleams off his bare back in the candlelight.

Suddenly, he makes a sickening gagging sound, and your breath catches in your throat. You see Mr. Bundinni toss his arm back behind him and dig his nails into the flesh of his back. He rakes his hand downward, blood pooling and spilling beneath his nails that look like claws in the dim light.

"What the…"

The words leave your mouth before you can even think about them. As soon as they escape into the air, Mr. Bundinni turns toward the door and looks right at you.

You've been caught. But what comes next is up to you.

*If you're feeling scared, close the door, go back to bed, and turn to **page 73***

*If you're feeling calm, stand firm by going to **page 31***

PAGE 30

The glass slips from your hand. It hits the bottom of the sink with a thud but luckily it doesn't break.

You turn around to find your grandmother standing behind you, hands on her hips and a scowl on her face.

"I said, what do you think you're doing?" she repeats.

"I-I—" you stammer.

Suddenly, her face lightens, and she smiles.

"You don't want that ol' water," she says. "Let me pour you a glass of Grandma's famous nitro lemonade."

She walks toward the fridge, then stops.

"Don't tell me you've forgotten about my lemonade," she says.

To be honest, you kinda had, but you don't want to let the old woman down. "No way!" you exclaim.

"Good, good," she says and finishes making her way to the fridge.

She pulls out a huge pitcher of bright yellow lemonade. She asks for the glass in the sink. You hand it to her, and she pours you the tallest glass of lemonade you've ever seen. It's practically overflowing when she hands it back to you.

"Guaranteed to quench any thirst," she says with a smile. And you know it's true.

Your grandma really is famous for the stuff. You can't remember how many times people have told her she should sell her recipe. She'd make more money than any bunny business ever could. But she's always respectfully said no. She likes her life just the way it is.

You start to bring the glass to your lips when the screaming starts.

---

*Find out what's going on by turning to **page 79***

"That you, kiddo?" you hear Mr. Bundinni say. His voice is mangled though. It sounds like he's smoked one hundred packs of cigarettes since dinner.

You pull open the door and take a step forward. Mr. Bundinni smiles at you. His eyes are yellow and jaundice looking. And it looks like he hasn't had a good shave in days.

"Are… are you okay?" you ask.

"No," Mr. Bundinni quickly, his voice dropping low. He lifts up an arm, and you hear a metal chain rattle. It takes you a moment, but you see the chain connects Mr. Bundinni's wrist to a nearby radiator. Your mind starts racing when he says, "I'm being held prisoner by your grandparents. Will you please help me?"

---

*If you're willing to help, go to **page 118***

*If you're not willing to help, go to **page 191***

PAGE 32

The shed is lit with dozens of black candles. Your grandparents stand holding the rabbit, as if waiting for something to happen. A shrine—an altar?—stands in the center of the small room. An old, wooden object is the centerpiece of the strange amalgam of candles, small bones, and plants. The wooden object appears carved. In the candlelight, you can see the features of a face etched into the woods—beady eyes, a small nose… and tall ears. Like a rabbit's ears.

Suddenly, Mr. Bundinni emerges from beyond the reach of the candles' light. He slides effortlessly across the room, as if floating. He takes the rabbit from your grandparents and turns to face the altar.

Through the window's glass, you hear his voice, but you have no idea what he's saying. It almost sounds like he's speaking a different language.

Mr. Bundinni lifts the rabbit above his head, shouts something, and then sets the rabbit on the altar. He produces a long, black knife out of nowhere. He holds the rabbit down and brings the knife towards it. You instinctively look away as the knife pierces flesh.

A moment later, you're able to bring yourself to look back into the shed.

You wish you hadn't though.

You watch as Mr. Bundinni, mouth smeared with black wetness, offers the rabbit's bleeding neck to your grandparents. Their mouths open, tongues flailing in an attempt to catch the rabbit's red life.

Turn to **page 138**

PAGE 33

Smalls invades your mind. His face flashes in your mind's eye, followed by terrible, terrible images. A world reborn through blood and fur. People locked in cramped cages. People like your grandpa. Your grandma. Ruled over by an army of mutant rabbits. Rabbits who torture. Who maim. Who kill…

You push back with your mind. You have to… fight… back. Try to force Smalls's images out. The drumbeat of pain increases with each passing second.

You see two options in your head. Revert Smalls back to a normal rabbit or end this once and for all.

Revert Smalls on **page 130**

End Smalls's reign of terror once and for all by turning to **page 13**

PAGE 34

You decide to follow the Rabbit Man.

The two of you slink through the woods, ducking low and hiding behind trees at random intervals. You can tell the Rabbit Man is hiding from something, but you're not sure what. When you ask about it, he replies in a whisper.

"The *other* players."

Curiosity gets the better of you. "Are they dressed up like rabbits too?"

The Rabbit Man nods. "Yeah, but not all rabbits are the same."

"What do you m—"

"We're here," he interrupts.

You come to a small clearing. It's perfectly still for a moment, then you see movement. Shadows emerge from the edge of the clearing. Heading straight for you.

Turn to **page 132**

You head to the living room with the shotgun. You set it aside as you sit down on the couch. Your instinct is to turn on the TV to help calm your mind, but you know you shouldn't. You can't get too distracted. Not while there's a were-rabbit on the loose.

A shiver runs up your spine as you feel dozens of beady, little eyes staring at you from all around the room. Your grandmother has quite the extensive collection of rabbit knickknacks and décor. They've always given you the creeps, but it's even worse now. You wonder if she'll get rid of any of it after a night like tonight.

A rabbit clock hangs on the wall, its ears tick-tocking with every passing second. Only a few more hours until daybreak.

If you can survive that long.

*See if you can make it through the night on **page 131***

PAGE 36

You wake up to the squeal of the cage's metal door opening. It takes you a second to remember where you are, how you got here. You hear voices, which only adds to the confusion. You recognize one of them as your grandpa's, but you can't place the others. One sounds like an older woman, and the other is younger, more high-pitched.

Suddenly, the round face of a little girl pops up in front of the cage. Her closeness frightens you. You try to scramble back farther into the corner of the cage, but there's nowhere to go.

"I want *that* one, Mommy!" the girl yells, worming a finger toward you through the gaps in the wire.

"Okay, honey," the woman's voice says. "We'll take it."

"Great!" your grandpa replies. "Let me just get it out of there for ya."

Your grandpa's large hand reaches into the cage and pulls you out. You feel free for a moment, just before he drops you into a small carrying cage. The lid on it snaps shut.

"Thanks for visiting Bunny Buddies Estates," your grandpa says. "Come back any time!"

As you're hoisted away toward a car you've never seen before, your grandpa's words echo in your tall, rabbit ears. Sadly, you know you won't be coming back any time soon. This is the end of one life and the start of a whole other one.

THE END...?

PAGE 37

You expect the bullets to start flying the moment your back is turned and you're running faster than you've ever run before. But you realize the Hare is smarter than that. He still has the cleaver, and he obviously knows how to use it. The image of the cop's severed head flashes in your mind. You can't let that happen to you.

You run until you come to a clearing in the woods. Your legs ache and your lungs burn, but you can't afford to waste time. The Hare could be—

Right behind you.

The smell of sweat and death wafts off his muscular body. You take a step back. And another. You'll only get one shot at this, so what's it going to be?

---

*Run. Go to **page 99***

*Try to reason with the Hare. Go to **page 141***

PAGE 38

The remainder of the summer drags on relatively uneventfully. You help your grandparents with the rabbits and various chores around the house, while getting the occasional day off. The nightly dinners don't change much with Mr. Bundinni gone, but you chalk some of that up to your grandparents not wanting to waste food. Still, a few weeks of eating carrots and celery gets old fast.

It's only about a month later that things get really odd. You notice your grandparents getting… hairier. It's like your grandpa hasn't shaved in weeks. And the hairs on your grandma's arms are so thick, you can barely see her skin. They shrug it off when you ask about it though. Nothing to worry about.

But you do worry. And your worrying is justified when on the night of a full moon, you see two huge rabbits roaming the yard.

You lock your bedroom door and crawl back to bed. Better get your rest, kiddo. In the morning, you've got a cure to start working on.

THE END

An hour later, you're back at your grandparents' house. The atmosphere is tense, but no one is really willing to risk interrupting your parents' vacation (that would make things *really* tense).

The summer drags on as you largely hide out in your room, away from your grandparents and Mr. Bundinni. As slow as it goes, the summer does eventually come to an end, and you head back home with your folks.

Your little misadventure at Bunny Buddies Estates may be miles behind you now, but something tells you it's not quite over. Whenever you're tempted to say something to your parents about it, you get this odd feeling you're being watched.

It couldn't possibly have anything to do with the dozens of bunnies constantly in the yard, could it?

THE END

"Smalls, please! You can't do this! My grandparents are still inside! You'll hurt them!"

"Better them than us," he says calmly.

"But they cared for you! The other rabbits too! Please!"

"Cared only long enough to exploit us. To use us. To profit off of us. No more. I've seen what's to come. I will not allow that to happen."

You fall to the ground, pleading, begging with Smalls. He closes his eyes and shuts out the world. As soon as he does, the house lets out one last mechanical shriek of fraying connections. And then, in total silence, the house flies up, up, up, and away. A trail of debris follows, like stardust behind a comet.

You never hear the crash of the house returning to Earth. It's been thrown too far away.

You look up at Smalls. He crosses the yard and begins opening cages. Rabbits hop out onto the ground one by one. As they dance around his feet, Smalls approaches where the house once stood.

"Good riddance."

THE END

PAGE 41

Something about this guy doesn't feel right (and it's not just the fact that he's wearing a bunny suit). You take a few steps back from him. The Rabbit Man tenses, as if ready to spring into action any minute. You stare each other down. And then finally, you make your move.

You break into a run, speeding away from the Rabbit Man. The dark forest whips around you. From behind you, you hear the Rabbit Man shout, "Be careful! Not all rabbits are the same!"

You have no idea what that means, but you don't turn back to ask. You keep running deeper into the woods until you're out of breath. Eventually, you collapse on the ground. The humid night air fills your lungs.

It's in between your pained gasps of air that you hear a burst of static and a familiar voice.

*Listen in on **page 106***

PAGE 42

"Easy way... please... sir."

The judge laughs heartily. "I like that. Respect. That's what you should have shown for your grandparents' private business—this town's private business—instead of spying. And out of respect for your grandparents who are pillars of our faith's community, we will indeed settle this the easy way. Exile. May Grandifal have mercy on your soul."

There's an audible gasp and a sudden surge of movement throughout the room.

"Judge, please, wait. Don't exile my grandchild," your grandma begs.

"My decision has been made," the judge replies. "Goodnight."

The judge manages to disappear into the darkness behind him. Two guards grab you by the arms and start to pull you away.

Exile yourself to **page 180**

PAGE 43

You're not scared of Bundinni. You look him dead in the eyes. "Tell. Me. Where. She. Is."

"Tell you?" Mr. Bundinni scoffs. "Why don't I just show you, kiddo?"

In one sweeping motion, he brings the bloody knife you stuck in his arm up to your face. He taps it to your nose and whispers words you can't understand.

Suddenly, a white light spreads across your face, blinding you. It consumes the room around you, engulfing it in light.

A moment passes, and when you can finally see again, you realize you're not in your grandparents' shed anymore.

Find out where you are on ***page 105***

PAGE 44

You decide to get something to drink. You leave your suitcase by the door and head to the kitchen.

It's a good-sized kitchen. And spotless. Just like your grandmother likes things.

You pull out a glass from one of the cabinets and fill it up with tap water from the sink. You guzzle it down quickly and then start to fill the glass up again.

You hear a soft creak behind you. Before you even have time to turn around, a voice rips through the room.

"WHAT DO YOU THINK YOU'RE DOING?"

---

*Turn around to **page 30***

PAGE 45

You point to the left. The cop pushes past you and heads down the path. You quickly follow behind.

The left path winds through the woods like a snake. It doesn't seem like you're getting any closer to getting out of here.

And then suddenly, the ground gives way, and you're falling down,

Down.

Down.

Fall to **page 19**

PAGE 46

You wake up in the dark. The air is thick and musty. You sit up and your head pounds. As your eyes slowly start to adjust to the darkness, you hear shuffling around you.

"You okay, kiddo?"

It's your grandpa.

"Where are we?" you ask.

"Down in the cellar. You've been out for a while. Maybe days. It's hard to tell down here. Things… things have changed a lot since then."

"What do you mean?"

"Smalls threw us down here. And… and he isn't alone anymore. There are more of his kind. More of those… *monster* rabbits. They're guarding the door, so we can't get out of here."

"Where's Grandma?"

"I don't know. Upstairs, I guess. I don't know what they want her for."

"It's the lemonade," you explain. "Her nitro lemonade. It does something to the rabbits. Makes them huge. Makes them stronger. Increases their brain power or something. Smalls wanted more of it. He said it was giving him visions and that he could read minds."

"But why didn't it affect us?"

"Maybe we didn't drink enough. Maybe it affects them differently because they're rabbits. I don't—"

Suddenly, the cellar doors heave open with an angry squeal. You're blinded as fresh sunlight pours in from the doorway. Heavy footsteps come right toward you.

---

*Turn to **page 161***

"I don't know about this," you say quickly.

The smile on Mr. Bundinni's face drops. He lets go of your shoulder and turns away from you. He picks up the knife off the table. "Oh, but you see, kiddo, you *do* know. And we can't have our little secret get out now, can we?"

"I promise I won't tell anyone!" you shout. You whip around to your grandparents, eyes begging them to do something, anything. They don't even dare to look at you.

"I know you won't, kiddo," Mr. Bundinni says. You turn back toward him to see him twisting the tip of the knife into the palm of his hand. Dark red blood spills out of the wound.

You decide to make a break for the door. You barrel toward it like a football player, but you're immediately stopped. Your grandparents grab you tightly by the arms, twist you back around to face Mr. Bundinni. You thrash to break free but can't. Your grandparents' grip on you is too strong.

Mr. Bundinni approaches. "You should have just taken our offer, kiddo."

He reaches toward you with his bloody hand. The world goes dark as he smears blood across your eyes.

Turn to **page 54**

PAGE 48

As soon as Mr. Bundinni disappears through the shattered remains of the window, your grandma is next to you, holding the shotgun. Your grandpa follows behind her and rushes to the window. He shakes his head.

"Think we got a problem," he mutters.

You lean over and look out the window to see what he means.

On the ground below, a small pool of blood gleams in the moonlight. But there's no Mr. Bundinni.

Your grandmother grabs you by the shoulder. Her grip is not kind or gentle. "Think it's time we had a little talk, kiddo."

Turn to ***page 171***

"Grandma, I let Smalls out of his cage the other day," you blurt out.

"What?" your grandma says.

"I let Smalls out. He was growing and growing inside his cage, and I just had to let him out. He ran away and now, he's huge. He's basically a monster. And he wants lemonade. Your lemonade. And he came here last night and threatened me, telling me I had to bring him more lemonade or else. And-and... And I don't know what to do!"

"Oh kiddo," she says. She wraps her arms around you and squeezes. "I think you've just been having nightmares. Maybe too much sun too. I know you city kids don't get outside much. Why don't you go lie down for a bit? Rest up. Don't worry about helping your grandpa with the rabbits today."

"I'm being serious, Grandma! Smalls was here, and he's huge! He wants lemonade!"

The concerned look on her face drops to one of annoyance.

"Now, kiddo, I won't tolerate any lying in my house. So, go on upstairs and get some rest. I'll call you down for lunch when it's ready."

"But—"

"No buts. Now, go."

*Slink upstairs by going to **page 61***

PAGE 50

You're a rabbit!

Your hands are gone, replaced with soft, little paws. Your arms, no, your whole body is covered in a layer of white fur. You dash over to the full-length mirror in the corner of the room. Your reflection only confirms what you've suspected.

Your ears are now tall and pointy. Your nose is now soft and pink. And your teeth!

You feel woozy. You step away from the mirror. This can't be happening. This has to be a dream.

You look yourself over again and this time you notice the cut on your paw-hand is still there. Yellow, oozing, and smelling of lemons.

Lemons. Your grandmother's lemonade! Maybe it had something to do with this. Why else would the cut smell like lemons? Maybe it somehow interacted with the rabbit bite and—

You know this is crazy. Stuff like this only happens in comic books and yet, here you are.

You've got to get out of this room. You have to find your grandmother. Have to find a way to turn yourself back to normal. But how?

You glance toward the closed bedroom door. You then look over at the window you opened earlier. Which one is it going to be?

If you use the door, go to **page 84**

If you go for the window, go to **page 121**

You meet your grandparents as you head back toward the house. Their eyes are wide with shock and concern.

You quickly rattle off something about an earthquake and cutting yourself on something as you tried to get out of the house. They don't seem to buy it at first, but once they see the mangled foundation, they change their tune.

The next day is mostly spent going over things with the insurance company. The house isn't really safe to go back into, so you spend most of the day outside. You kill the time until your parents come to pick you up by reading and taking walks with your grandma.

The walks are nice, but you can't shake the feeling that no matter where you go, someone is watching you from deep within the woods.

THE END

PAGE 52

You duck behind a tree. It's not the greatest of hiding places, but it'll do.

From your hiding place, you watch your grandparents remove one of the rabbits from its cage. With it, they head toward the shed even farther back on the property. The shed is nestled close to the tree line of the woods, which looks especially dark tonight. But the shed is lit up for some reason. A stale orange light wobbles from within it. You watch as your grandparents go inside.

You quickly sneak across the yard. You slide up against the shed's wall and poke your head up to a window.

You cannot believe what you find inside.

Go to **page 32**

PAGE 53

Your heart thuds in your chest as you try to stand perfectly still. You can't risk waking up your grandparents. Not now. Not when you're so close to freeing Mr. Bundinni.

Luckily, the two of them start to snore again. You breathe a sigh of relief. They're still asleep.

Time to get out of here.

You make your way back to Mr. Bundinni's room. He's so glad to see you.

You immediately rush over and start trying out the various keys on the handcuffs. There must be a dozen there, so it takes a little bit of trial and error.

As you test the keys though, you notice something odd about the handcuffs. They don't look like the ones you've seen in police movies. They're heavy and have some sort of paint on them. Intricate symbols of some kind.

A chill runs through your body. Maybe you shouldn't be doing this. Maybe there's a reason Mr. Bundinni is handcuffed to the radiator, you realize.

Just as this dawns on you though, you hear a click. And the handcuffs fall to the floor.

*Go to **page 194***

PAGE 54

You wake up inside a cage surrounded by the smell of rabbits. You run to the cage wall and shake it with furry paws.

Wait. Furry paws?

Oh, no! You're a rabbit!

You race around the cage on your little rabbit legs, trying to find a way out, but come up short.

Soon, your grandparents come out and feed you. You don't know if it's because of your new rabbit eyes or what, but they look more youthful and energetic than ever.

"We're sorry, kiddo," they say as they drop food pellets into your cage.

But you know they're not. They allowed this to happen, and now, you're stuck waiting for the day you're sacrificed.

THE END

You don't get much rest in your room. You feel guilty about losing Smalls, but what else were you supposed to do? He was suffering, practically about to explode in that cage of his. Maybe if you just told your grandpa what happened, he'd understand.

Understand what though? That Smalls quadrupled in size in a matter of hours? That he could somehow talk? No way he'd believe you. You could hardly believe it yourself.

Eventually, your grandma knocks on the door and asks if you can help your grandpa with the rabbits. You're tired, but you say sure and meet him outside.

Your grandpa is still in a pretty sour mood over losing Smalls, but you can tell he appreciates the help. And it feels kinda nice to do it. In your own little way, it's like you're making up for what happened to Smalls.

While you're feeding the rabbits, your grandpa heads inside to grab some lemonade. As you pour rabbit food into the dispensers, an odd feeling creeps up your back. It feels like you're being watched. You turn ever so slightly.

The yard is empty. There's no one around.

Then it hits you. Of course you're being watched. You're standing in front of a cage full of hungry rabbits, their beady little eyes all focused on you. You chuckle to yourself.

But that uneasy feeling doesn't go away.

*Go to **page 9***

PAGE 56

You join the other two rabbits. You stare down at the pellets before you. Are you really about to eat rabbit food?

Just then, your stomach grumbles. You realize you haven't eaten anything since getting to your grandparents'. Maybe... maybe it'll be okay?

You take a tiny nibble of a pellet. You expect it to taste disgusting, but instead your mouth fills with flavor. Rich, delicious flavor. You take another bite and then another. Soon, you're wolfing down pellet after pellet after pellet.

"Whoa! Slow down there, new guy!" one of the rabbits says.

"Yeah, otherwise, you're going to explode!" says the other one, but you're too busy to care.

You keep eating and eating. You eat until all the pellets are gone. After thoroughly licking the trough, you take a step back. The other rabbits look on in horror at you.

You slink back to the corner of the cage, embarrassed. But you're even more sleepy. You start to nod off...

Turn to **page 36**

You come crashing down onto Grandifal's homeworld a moment later (emphasis on the crashing down part). Your legs break from the fall, but not all hope is lost.

Your sudden appearance draws the attention of the locals, who happen to be humanoid rabbit creatures. They bring you back to their warren, where they tend to your injuries.

A few days, weeks, or maybe months go by, you have no idea. All you know is that one night, you're carried out on a stretcher to an open field to meet Grandifal, the Great Rabbit.

Well, meet is a loose term. It's more like gaze upon Him in awe… and madness. Because Grandifal was never meant to be seen by mortal *human* eyes. His greatness is too much for you to bear. Something inside your brain, your mind, and perhaps even your soul, snaps. You're never the same after that.

You live out your few remaining days wandering and screaming in the fields, until one of your "neighbors" finally gets tired of you waking them up too early in the morning. Then something inside of you really does snap (your spine) and it's…

THE END

PAGE 58

You take a few bites of pancake and down the glass of lemonade. You quickly get dressed and head downstairs. The first floor is quiet for a moment, but there's something else too. Anticipation?

"Grandma?" you call out.

"In the living room, kiddo."

You head into the living room and can't believe what you find there.

Turn to **page 185**

PAGE 59

You're back at your grandparents' house. You turn back toward the cop. But how did he know this was the house? You didn't even mention Bunny Buddies Estates.

"Do… you know about this?" you ask.

"I think we need to talk," the cop says.

Fuck that. You're out of the car in a flash. You start sprinting through the yard.

"HEY! GET BACK HERE!" the cop roars from the car.

You keep running though. There's no way you're gonna stop now.

Suddenly, the crack of a gunshot echoes through the night air. You throw yourself to the ground. You feel fine, but you know adrenaline can be one hell of a drug. You pat yourself down, looking for blood, looking for a bullet hole. You don't find any. You turn to see the cop jogging toward you, gun in hand. You don't have any time to waste.

You hop back on your feet. You scan the area looking for a place to go. A place to hide. Two options creep into your mind.

---

*Run into the woods on **page 147***

*Run toward the shed on **page 168***

PAGE 60

"Well, how did you get in here, little fella?" your grandma says as she looks down at you. She then looks around the room and calls your name.

You hop toward her, frantically hoping she'll put it all together.

"It's me!!!" you yelp.

Your grandma doesn't seem to hear you. She only looks down at you and smiles. "Aww. You probably want to go back to your friends, huh?"

"What? No! It's me! I've turned into a rabbit! I need help!"

Your grandmother picks you up and carries you out of the room. You head down the stairs and into the kitchen. On the counter, you spot a tall pitcher filled with lemonade. You try to squirm toward it, thinking maybe it'll help change you back, but you're too slow. Your grandma carries you outside. She walks through the yard and to the rabbit cages. A wire door squeals open, and you're quickly thrown inside. You leap for the door, just in time for it to close on your little rabbit face.

You're trapped.

Go to **page 204**

You spend the rest of the day in your room, except for lunch and dinner. And even then, you wish you were up in your room. If there's any piece of your story that Grandma bought, it was the part about you letting Smalls out of his cage. Neither one of your grandparents will look at you.

It's a crummy day, made worse by the evening. You know you have to meet Smalls, so you head down to the kitchen to grab some lemonade. Unfortunately, when you get there, the pitcher is empty.

Just your luck.

You venture outside toward the dark woods. You're not sure where Smalls is, but you feel like you're being watched.

Turns out you are. Smalls quickly emerges from the woods.

He looks bigger than he did last night. At least in the head. It looks swollen, bulging in strange places. One eye looks huge and ready to pop out of his skull.

"Where is it?" he shouts. He grabs you by the shirt and lifts you off the ground.

"I-I don't have any! I wasn't able to ask about the recipe, and there's none left."

The rabbit's eyes dart back and forth, scanning your face.

"I can read your mind," he says. "I know you're telling the truth. So, you have one last chance. Are you going to help me or not?"

---

*Help Smalls on **page 23***

*Refuse on **page 160***

PAGE 62

Bundinni looks deadly serious. You shrink away from him, away from the ashes.

A smile creeps across his face. "That's what I thought."

You look back toward your grandpa. He's pressed up against the shed wall. His mouth hangs open; his face is stunned with shock. His eyes don't leave the pile of ashes on the floor. You know he won't be able to help you.

You turn back towards Mr. Bundinni as he begins to speak.

"You've already messed up my plans once, but I won't allow you to do it again. The woman was a good worker. Capable and willing." He nods to the ashes. "I guess you'll just have to pick up the slack. Or else."

Go to **page 163**

PAGE 63

You scramble off the ground and say, "Oh my gosh, I'm so glad to see you!"

You walk toward the Rabbit Man, who is standing beside a tall tree. As you approach though, the Rabbit Man walks—no, *glides*, the movement too perfectly smooth—behind the tree. You stop.

A shiver runs up your spine. Something about this doesn't feel right.

You come around to the back of the tree, but the Rabbit Man is no longer there. You turn to the left and right, catching a glimpse of the Rabbit Man moving through the woods. Moving around you. Silently circling you.

"C'mon, man," you say with a shaky voice. "This isn't funny anymore. Let's get out of here."

The forest freezes for a split second, and then...

SNAP!

You whirl around to the sound of a twig breaking and come face-to-face with the rabbit. It's then you realize this isn't the Rabbit Man you met earlier.

This is someone else.

This is a Rabbit Woman.

Go to **page 122**

You grip the gun tighter and mentally prepare yourself to use it.

Luckily, you don't have to.

Your grandparents emerge from the woods, just like they said they would. They look upset, but at least they're still alive.

Your grandpa grumbles on the way back to the house about not being fast enough to chase after Bundinni. Your grandmother only shakes her head.

"So, what do we do now?" you ask when you're finally in the safe confines of the kitchen.

"We wait," your grandma says just as the sun starts to creep up past the tree line. "We wait for another full moon. He'll be back. They *always* come back."

Betcha didn't think you'd be hunting were-rabbits this summer, did ya kiddo?

PAGE 65

"I'll stay here," you say.

"That's a good choice, kiddo," your grandfather says. "Here. Take this."

He hands you one of the freshly loaded shotguns. You're about to reject it when he gives you a hard look and eases it into your hands. The gun feels heavy and cold like death.

"It's just in case," he says. "We'll be back by daybreak. Love you, kiddo."

You follow your grandparents to the front door. Without another word, they disappear into the night, leaving you all alone.

Turn to **page 35**

PAGE 66

One of the cages is filled to the brim with brown fur. *Smalls*.

But he's not small anymore. He's tripled, no, quadrupled in size. His face is smashed up against the cage's wire walls. His beady eyes are wider than you've ever seen on a rabbit. And then, he cries.

The sound is strangely guttural. Primal. He's clearly in pain.

You look around the yard, toward the house. How could your grandparents not hear this?

Smalls shrieks again, and you see his body struggle to free itself from the cage's confines. You hear a sick squelching sound come from the cage. A foot shoots out from between two wires and appears to grow.

He's outgrowing the cage, but it's holding on tight to him. Wrapping around him. Strangling him.

Quick! You've got to do something!

… Right?

Let Smalls out of the cage on **page 134**

Do nothing and turn to **page 18**

PAGE 67

Are you nuts? This creature is HUGE! And you think it's a good idea to confront it? What are you going to do? Hit it with a plastic spatula? No way!

*Stay hidden and head over to **page 150***

PAGE 68

"What's going on? I thought you were going to help me!" you shout as you're pushed through the police station and out the main door. You're shoved into the back of a police car, and a black hood is thrown over your face. You can't see anything through it, and it smells musky. Like it's recently been used.

You hear the car turn on and can feel it start to move. You have no idea where you're going, but you know it isn't good. You curse yourself for telling the truth.

Sometime later, the car stops, and you hear the driver get out. Before you know it, you're being pulled out of the car and shoved forward. The hood stays on, and your feet scrape across rough concrete. Judging by the squeaking of hinges and slams, you're taken through a series of doors. The air gets colder too, so you know you're inside somewhere.

Where are they taking me? you wonder.

As if on cue, the hood comes off and you're shocked by who you see.

---

*Find out who is there by going to **page 6***

Within just a few heartbeats, the massive form is upon you. It leaps into the air, and time slows to a drip. It's another rabbit-clad player, this one a hulking behemoth of muscles and ripped costume fur. He almost seems to float in the air as you make eye contact with him.

Then suddenly, time speeds back up too fast, like it's making up for lost time. You struggle to comprehend what you're seeing. There's a slit of silver, of metal in the moonlight. A swift slash. A wet noise. A wetter spray across your face. A soft thud.

You wipe the warm wetness from your eyes. Your hands come back red and smeared. You see the giant rabbit in front of you. A bloody cleaver is in his hand and the cop's severed head is at his feet.

*Go to **page 135***

PAGE 70

You rush out of your room and into the hallway. You have to see if anyone is hurt.

You're about to run into Mr. Bundinni's room when a figure exits the room. You crash into them, but they manage to stand firm. They grab you, twist you around, and jab something into your neck.

The world fades to black.

*Turn to **page 107***

Yeah, that'll work, you think.

You press yourself against the cage wall and then launch yourself at the opposing wall. You turn yourself into a spring, bouncing off wall after wall. Back and forth you run, sending the other two rabbits racing away from you. The jostling of the metal cage is a nice benefit, but not enough to get your grandparents' attention you decide. You start screaming in your rabbit voice, hoping it'll pull one of them in.

And the crazy thing is, it seems to work!

After just a few whirlwind moments spent running around the cage, you see your grandpa come out of the house. You don't stop running though. Not yet. Not until he has opened the cage door.

But he never does. Instead, you hear him call out your name. Not once or twice, but over and over. You hear the concern grow in his voice as he paces the yard.

You press yourself up against the wire frame of the cage and scream with all your might. "I'm right here, Grandpa! I'm right here!"

He clearly doesn't hear you or at least doesn't understand your rabbit tongue. He heads back toward the house. He meets your grandmother by the door, holds her arm, and nods gently. They go back inside.

*Go to **page 197***

PAGE 72

You struggle to break free, but the shadow is stronger than you are. It covers your mouth with some kind of cloth and hisses in your ear. No, not hisses. Shushes.

"Shut up, or you'll get us both caught!" the voice says in the same strained whisper as earlier.

Us?

You slowly stop struggling. You feel whoever has a hold of you ease up too. A threshold is reached, and you manage to break free. You turn around to face whoever grabbed you, ready to fight them if need be. You're shocked at what you see.

Turn to **page 90**

You close Mr. Bundinni's door and rush back to your room. You slink under the covers on your bed. Your heart races, and one thought dominates your mind.

Hesawmehesawmehesawmehesawme

Your bedroom door creaks open. Your throat tightens and your heart stops for a beat before shifting into maximum overdrive.

You see Mr. Bundinni take a step into your room.

"You shouldn't have gone into my room, *kiddo*." His voice is loud, angry, distorted.

He takes another step and then another. He steps into the moonlight pouring in from the window and begins his transformation.

Witness the transformation on **page 145**

PAGE 74

"Are you really suggesting we take the kid hostage?" Warren questions.

"It's our best bet," Jim says. "They won't hurt their own grandkid. Besides, this sure beats the hell out of waiting and seeing if someone comes and tries to kill us."

The others take a moment to consider their options. Then, a silent agreement is made. Your fate is sealed.

Turn to **page 203**

"Your... *family*..." he repeats. "This... *this* is where it all starts."

"Where what all starts, Smalls? What are you talking about?"

"The *massacre*. I-I can't allow that to happen. I can't allow them to die like that," he says, seeming to ignore you.

"Die?!" The word cracks in your voice. "Who is going to die, Smalls? Who?"

"Not them, not my brethren," he says. "Not if I can stop them."

"Stop who, Smalls? What is going on? Please just tell me! Maybe I can help!"

"No, you'll only try to help *them*," he accuses.

He looks right at you. And this time, you know it.

In a flash, Smalls runs his paw over your stomach and darts past you.

You feel a strange warmth blossom through your shirt. You touch it lightly and your hand comes away dark, wet, and warm. Blood.

You turn the direction that Smalls ran. You see his massive form bounding over to your grandparents' house.

Go to **page 202**

PAGE 76

You sit as still as possible, begging the darkness to conceal your presence.

But then the lights come on.

Bundinni is standing by the door. Covered in fur and blood. In his hands—his paws—he holds two severed heads.

Your grandparents. Their faces twisted in terror.

He drops them to the floor.

"Your turn, *kiddo*."

Bundinni starts to walk toward you. You lift the gun, but it's heavy and awkward in your hands. It doesn't matter anyway. Bundinni knocks it away from you with one powerful swipe.

Bundinni was wrong though. It's not your turn. It's his. And he's about to end this game.

You've been waiting by the door for about a minute when you hear voices. You take a step farther into the house, and the floorboards creak beneath your sneakers. Immediately, the voices stop and so do you.

A strained silence fills the house.

"That you, kiddo?" an elderly woman's voice calls from another room.

"Yeah, it's me, Grandma," you reply.

You start heading toward the room her voice was coming from when bam! She's right in front of you. Her smile is as wide as can be. Without warning, she wraps you in a big hug. She practically lifts you off the ground, and she's squeezing you so tight, it's hard to breathe.

"It's so nice to have you here, kiddo," she says, setting you back down on the floor.

Since when did your grandmother get so strong? you wonder.

"Nice to see you too, Grandma. Is Grandpa in there? I want to say hi."

"Oh, no. He's out back with the rabbits."

"But I thought I heard voices? Were you talking to someone on the phone?"

"Oh, I must have forgotten to tell you," she says, but you can already hear the footsteps approaching. "We have an extra special guest staying with us this summer."

*Find out who it is by going to **page 28***

PAGE 78

You're tempted to run, but you know that'd only make things worse. You're led back to the police car, and you're surprised when the cop opens the front passenger side door for you. You thought for sure he'd throw you in the back. You slide inside the car.

A minute later, you're riding down the bumpy, gravel road.

"So, where you from, kid?"

You don't say a word.

"C'mon. You got to give me something to work with," the cop pleads. "Can you tell me anything?"

Oh boy, do you have something to tell him. But you're not sure if it's the right time to reveal your grandparents'—no, *Mr. Bundinni's*—secrets.

You look over the cop. He looks at you. It's now or never. What's it going to be?

Keep up the silent act on **page 101**

Spill your guts on **page 12**

Well, screaming may be a bit of an exaggeration. It's more like angry shouting.

Your grandma rushes over to the sink, and you move aside, careful not to spill any of the lemonade she just poured you. She leans over the sink and peers out the window into the backyard.

"Oh, he's done it again, that man," she says. "Go see if your grandpa needs help with those rabbits. Looks like they're loose again."

You look down at the glass of lemonade and then back at her.

"Hurry!" she says. "You can take the lemonade with you, just don't spill any!"

What are you going to do?

*If you decide to down the glass of lemonade right then and there, go to **page 100***

*If you take it with you, go to **page 81***

PAGE 80

What could they possibly be doing outside at night? Is there some kind of emergency with the rabbits? Maybe you better go see if they need some help.

You don't bother slipping on a pair of shoes. You head outside in your bare feet.

You start to approach your grandparents, who are now near the rabbit cages, fiddling with the metal contraptions. They're talking in quick, hushed tones that are impossible to understand.

Something about this seems off, you think. You're not sure what though. Maybe there really is an emergency with one of the rabbits and that's what's throwing off the vibes.

Still, you stop yards away from your grandparents. What are you going to do?

---

*Ask if they need help on **page 162***

*Continue to watch secretly on **page 52***

Your grandma rushes you out of the kitchen. "Go! Go!"

You grip your glass of lemonade tight, but it's already getting slippery with condensation. You make your way outside through a side door.

In the backyard, you find your grandpa and several empty rabbit cages. Brown and white rabbits bounce around the yard.

"Hey kiddo! Help me with these rabbits, will ya? They're making a jail break!"

You crack a smile. He always calls you kiddo, no matter how old you get.

You walk towards him when suddenly something shoots in between your feet. You stumble and fall. The glass of lemonade tumbles from your hand and shatters on the concrete slab patio next to the house.

Your grandpa rushes over and helps you up. "You okay, kiddo? Glass didn't cut ya, did it?"

"No, I'm fine," you say.

You turn to find a white rabbit with gray spots not far from you. Its nose twitches, but the rabbit doesn't move.

"Ol' Gonzo is a tricky one," your grandpa says. "He's the brains of the operation. Masterminded their whole escape, ya know. Might take two of us to catch him."

You can't tell if your grandpa is joking or if he's just spent too much time with the rabbits.

"You go that way," he says. "And I'll go this way, and we'll grab him in the middle."

You take your starting position. So does your grandpa. You take a slow step forward. Then another. And another.

---

*Meet in the middle on **page 27***

PAGE 82

The night is alive all around you. You hear the far-off hooting of owls and the sharp chirps of crickets. Bugs of all kinds swarm your ankles. You'll have more than a few mosquito bites by morning… if you live that long.

You try to swallow down your fear, but it keeps threatening to come back up and spew all over you.

Just a little longer, you tell yourself. They said they'd be right back. Can't be too much longer, can it?

You pace the same small patch of grass where your grandparents left you. You keep the shotgun pointed at the ground. You don't know what you'd do if you actually had to point that thing at someone… or something.

As if on cue, a twig snaps within the woods in front of you. You hear footsteps. Quick, heavy footsteps. Coming right for you!

What do you do?

---

*Fire the gun! No were-rabbit is getting you tonight! Turn to **page 187***

*Or you can wait a second to see what's coming by going to **page 64***

The world around you freezes, but the sound of the gunshot echoes in your ears. Then, all at once, things move fast and slow.

Your grandma crumples to the ground.

Your grandpa lunges toward her, his motion blurring and doubling before your eyes.

The Hare's gun tumbles out of his hand.

And then the Hare falls too.

Blood pours out of a bullet hole in the center of his back.

You turn around—slowly? Or so fast the world around you blurs?—and see Mr. Bundinni standing behind you, gun in hand.

"I hate cheaters," he says.

Turn to ***page 94***

PAGE 84

You decide to try to use the door. It's shut so you make a leap for the doorknob. You jump and bump into the metal knob several times but make no progress actually opening the door.

You decide to try a different route to opening the door. You slide a paw under the door and attempt to pull it loose. You're able to shake the door a little but not open it.

You soon realize your best bet is to try to get someone to open the door for you. You back away from the door, take a running charge, and smash right into it. Pain surges through your little bunny body, but you've managed to make quite a thump. Hopefully, it'll be enough to get someone's attention.

You charge again and again, thumping against the door each time. You soon feel bruised and beaten and exhausted. You're about to give up when you hear the whine of someone coming up the stairs. Their steps get louder and louder. Closer and closer.

You have one more chance. You take a flying leap at the door. You crash into it and fall to the floor. You take a heavy breath as the door opens.

Go to **page 60**

PAGE 85

You know how to play this game. You've seen your parents do it before. You cross your arms over your chest and refuse to say another word.

A moment passes.

"The strong silent type, eh?" the judge says. "I can work with that. Case dismissed."

"But Judge!" Mr. Bundinni shouts. "The child has seen things! They risk exposing our community's secrets! Grandifal forbid the child open their mouth and—"

"Silence, Bundinni!" the judge booms. "I trust this matter is resolved. The child will not say a word. I *guarantee* it."

Turn to **page 39**

PAGE 86

Your grandmother brings you back to her camp, which consists of a firepit and a makeshift mattress. She tells you about what's happened since Bundinni sent her here. She's stayed roughly in the same spot, in case someone else came here looking for her. That's how she found you. It's been years of rough living, she estimates.

When you tell her that only a few minutes passed between you and her getting sent here, a tear rolls down her cheek.

"Time moves differently here, I gather," she says.

"Where is here exactly?" you ask.

"The home dimension of Mr. Bundinni's rabbit god, Grandifal," she answers. "I've been studying this world. Figuring out how it all works. The only thing I haven't managed to do is make my famous nitro lemonade recipe."

You laugh, and the mood feels lighter for a brief moment. The sky is getting dark though, and your grandmother says it's time for bed. You close your eyes and drift off to sleep.

Wake up on **page 20**

The cop's footsteps move away from you.

You wait for him to pass you by. Even then, when you're sure he's gone, you wait just to be absolutely certain. You pick yourself off the ground and start running.

One thing you hadn't counted on when you decided to stay in the woods is that you don't know these woods very well. And it's dark. So, you run as best you can. But you never do see that tripwire coming. As you get snagged on it and fly through the air, you fall into a pit of sharp, wooden spikes.

As you bleed out on the spikes, you realize this game is real. And you just lost.

PAGE 88

You grab ahold of the knife. A surge of electricity courses through you.

The rabbit nuzzles up against your chest. The candlelight dances in its eyes.

There's no way you can kill the rabbit in your arms. But you've got to do something.

So, you lift the knife. Your aim is wild, but you stab Mr. Bundinni. He reels back and screams, the knife now sticking out of his arm.

When he looks back at you, his eyes are fire.

"You really shouldn't have done that, kiddo," he growls.

His voice drops, and he begins to mutter something under his breath. Words you can't begin to understand. They come fast and heavy, slick with contempt.

Mr. Bundinni rips the knife out of his arm, points it at you, and screams the final words of his incantation. A purple light jets out from the tip of the knife, barreling towards you.

You get a glance of Mr. Bundinni's surprised face when your grandmother steps in front of you.

*Go to **page 17***

It doesn't take long for more police officers to arrive (apparently, it was a slow night). Once backup arrives, your grandparents and Mr. Bundinni are shoved into the back of a few police cars and taken away. They have charges pending for animal cruelty as well as child endangerment and neglect.

They're not happy about having their vacation interrupted, but your parents agree to come pick you up in the morning. You stay at the police station overnight.

The cop who picked you up tells you it's difficult what happened, but you did the right thing. Apparently, Bundinni was behind it all and convinced your grandparents his strange "eating habits" would keep them alive longer.

You're not sure in your heart of hearts that having your grandparents arrested was exactly the right thing to do, but you're glad this story is finally over.

THE END

PAGE 90

The person who grabbed you is wearing a rabbit costume. Head-to-toe, they're decked out in white furry fabric that looks like it's been through the wringer. The costume is torn in various spots, and dirt mars the fabric. A necklace is wrapped around his neck with a lone rabbit's foot looped on it.

"Why-why are you wearing... *that*?" you ask.

"I could ask you the same thing," the rabbit shoots back. "Where's your costume?"

"I-I don't have one? Why would I need one?"

You see the Rabbit Man's shoulders sag. "Oh shit. You're not with the game, are you?"

"What game?"

"*The* game!" he says. He takes a step back from you. "Fuck! I thought you looked weird when I grabbed you. I thought maybe we could work together. Fuck this game, man!"

"What are you talking about? What game?!"

"You really don't know? Shit, you're in for a wild night. If you can survive it."

*Go to **page 4***

"Don't worry. I'm not going to kill you," Smalls says with a grin. "Not yet anyway."

You try to catch your breath. You hear your heart booming in your ears.

No. Wait.

It's not your heart. It's footsteps. Coming *down* the stairs.

You turn toward the hall doorway, ready to scream, but your grandparents are already there.

"What in the hell is—"

The words die in your grandpa's throat as Smalls punches him in the face. The rabbit's furry fist sends your grandpa's head smack-dab into the kitchen wall. He crumbles to the ground, and your grandma screams like you've never heard anyone scream before.

Smalls turns to you with another sinister grin. "Why do I need you when I can go straight to the source?!"

"Grandma!" you scream. "Runnnnnn!"

But your grandma is too busy screaming to hear your warning. And before you know it, Smalls lifts one of his massive feet. It kicks out toward you, sending you shooting across the room.

You thump against the wall, and everything goes black.

Go to page 46

Without another word, two officers grab you and escort you out of the room. You glare one final time at your grandparents, but they just stare on. You can't tell if it's shock or apathy on their faces.

You're led through a series of hallways to a large room. It's empty as far as you can tell. The officers shove you forward.

"It's hungry tonight," one of them says as they close the door to the room.

You're looking around the room, searching for a way out, when suddenly the floor gives way. You fall through the opening in the floor into a pit below. It's dark and musky.

You barely have time to gather your senses when you see movement around you. A white, furry mass approaches you, the musky stench growing stronger.

With each booming step, the figure becomes clearer. It's a giant rabbit. Its eyes are wild, red, and rabid. Its front teeth are as big as a chainsaw blade.

As it looms over you, you squeak out, "You're not a vegetarian, are you?"

PAGE 93

You slink over to the corner of the cage. You have to figure a way out of here.

Your eyes are dead set on the cage door. It's the most obvious way out, but perhaps a complicated one. Maybe you could flip the latch somehow?

Or maybe you could chew through the metal of the cage? Rabbits have strong teeth, right?

Or maybe your best bet is to get someone to let you out of the cage? You could cause a commotion perhaps? It worked getting you out of the bedroom after all.

You mull it over for a few minutes before deciding to...

---

*Attempt to unlock the cage door on **page 167***

*Chew through the cage on **page 113***

*Cause a ruckus on **page 71***

PAGE 94

You rush over to your grandparents. Luckily, your grandma is fine. Startled, but fine. Due to Mr. Bundinni's crack shot, the Hare never had the chance to pull the trigger.

Once everything is calmed back down, your grandparents and Mr. Bundinni explain what happened tonight.

Turns out running a rabbit farm isn't as profitable as it used to be. Your grandparents fell on hard times, and Mr. Bundinni approached them with a business opportunity. In exchange for running a dark web survive-the-night game on their property, your grandparents (and the cash-strapped police department) would be handsomely compensated.

They never expected you to find out about the game, since it was meant to be played at night and deep within the woods. They even explained that the blood-drinking you saw in the shed was fake. All meant to drive up views for the real carnage of the night.

The story is incredible, almost unbelievable. But then again, you've seen things tonight that you'd never imagined you would.

As morning breaks, you're just glad you and your grandparents are safe and sound.

That is, until round two next week.

PAGE 95

You slip on your shoes and head outside. The sound becomes much clearer out there. It's coming from the backyard.

With every step you take, the sound gets louder. But you hear more than that. It's not just loud, it's emotional. *Painful*. Whatever is making the noise is in agony.

You near the rabbit cages. By then, it's clear that's where the sound is coming from. You slowly approach one of the cages and gasp.

*Turn to **page 66***

PAGE 96

"Don't hurt the kid!" your grandmother yells. She tries to come toward you, but Mr. Bundinni pushes her back.

"Oh, you have worse things coming to you, my dear," he growls at her.

The next thing you know, Bundinni hoists you up by your shirt and drags you outside. He marches you around the side of the house and throws open the cellar door. He tosses you down into the cellar. When he slams the door shut, you're plunged into darkness.

Despite not being able to see a thing, you can still hear what's going on above you. You hear your grandparents' screams as Bundinni tortures them for the trouble you've caused. The screaming and shouting go on for what seems like hours until suddenly... they stop.

Slow, purposeful footsteps cross the floorboards above you and exit the house. You hear the faint start of a car engine and the crunch of speeding tires on gravel. Then... nothing.

You estimate you have a couple days left before you die of thirst. You just hope someone shows up before then.

THE END

PAGE 97

The inside of the shed is lit by a host of red candles. They're scattered throughout the room, casting throbbing light around. Mr. Bundinni stands in the middle of the room, next to a table with an odd assortment of items on it. It's covered in a blood red cloth. The skull of a small rabbit rests in the middle of the table. A knife and two small cages with live rabbits are there too.

"What is all of this?" you ask.

Your grandparents push you farther into the shed and close the door behind them.

"What do you know about rabbits, kiddo?" your grandpa asks.

"Rabbits? I dunno. What-what's going on?"

Mr. Bundinni approaches you. He rests a large hand on your shoulder.

"Did you know that rabbits represent fertility and prosperity in certain cultures?" he says. "That they are a symbol for life renewed?"

You look back at your grandparents. "What is he talking about?"

Mr. Bundinni squeezes your shoulder, drawing your attention back to him. "I'm talking about life. And how we can ensure yours never ends."

Go to **page 140**

"Kiddo, is that you?"

"Grandma?"

Your grandmother emerges from the shadows, accompanied by a massive rabbit. It's nearly as big as she is, and stranger yet, it looks to be wearing some kind of makeshift saddle. But it's your grandma that's the real sight to see.

Her hair is long, gray, and wild. Rivers of wrinkles run across her tanned face. And her outfit. She's covered in patches of fur hides. You can't help but think she kinda looks like a mighty Amazon warrior from a 1950s movie.

You rush over, desperately wanting to hug her. Your grandmother gestures for you to slow down, and the rabbit behemoth behind her lets out an uneasy squeal.

"Careful there, kiddo," she says. "You don't want to scare Bertha here."

"Bertha?"

Your grandmother smiles and you get the sense that it's the first time she's smiled in a long time.

She wraps an arm around you. "C'mon, let's chat."

---

*Catch up with your grandma on **page 86***

PAGE 99

The Hare smiles, and you break out into a run.

Halfway across the clearing, you turn back to see if he's chasing you. He's not. But something else is. Something shiny in the moonlight. Something spinning toward you.

It collides with you. You tumble through the air. Crash onto the hard ground.

A moment later, you sit up, dizzy, the world spinning. You try to get your bearings, but your vision is split in two. It's like something is wedged between your eyes. It takes you a moment to realize that something *is* wedged between your eyes.

A hand—your hand?—feels the cleaver sticking out of your head, bisecting your face. Warmth spills across your cheeks. Angry, red warmth. *Blood.*

Your vision starts to blur and darken around the edges, but you see the Hare approaching. He reaches down, tugs on the cleaver. With a wet snap, everything goes dark.

THE END

PAGE 100

You gulp down the lemonade as fast as you can and set the glass aside. Immediately, you feel woozy as the sugar rushes to your head.

You go outside and the humid air greets you by clinging to your skin. You find your grandpa still grappling with the army of loose rabbits in the backyard. He immediately starts barking orders.

"Get that one! Quick!" he says, pointing to a gray and white rabbit.

You scoop it up in your arms. A second later, you feel the rabbit bite down on your hand.

You let out a short yelp and drop the rabbit.

"Did it bite ya?" your grandpa asks.

"Yeah, I think so."

You wave your hand in the air, trying to shake out the pain, but it doesn't go away. You and your grandpa look at the bite wound. It's pretty big. Who knew rabbits had *that* big of teeth? But what's stranger than the size of the bite is the color. It's not red or bleeding like you'd expect. Instead, the wound is neon yellow with a clear ooze seeping out.

"Do you think it's infected?" you ask.

"Too early for that," your grandpa replies. "But better be safe than sorry. Head inside and have your grandma clean it up."

Do as your grandpa says and head to **page 175**

You don't trust this guy. You cross your arms, push back into the seat, and stare out the window (not that there's much to see on a dusty road in the middle of the night).

"Okay, have it your way," the cop says.

A while later, you arrive in a small nearby town. The cop pulls into the police station. Before you can get out, he's by your door. He opens it for you and leads you inside the station. There, he drops you off with some folks at the front desk.

"Runaway from the looks of it. Found the kid on Route 9," the cop says to one of the people at the desk.

"We'll take it from here," a lady with a beehive haircut says. "Thanks, Officer Charleston."

Charleston tips his hat and heads back out into the night.

*Go to **page 177***

"That's okay," you say. "I'm already up. I can help."

Your grandparents' faces drop.

"Kid was bound to find out sooner or later," your grandpa says to your grandma.

"Find out what?" you ask.

"C'mon, kiddo," you grandpa says, motioning for you to come to him.

You cross the yard to join your grandparents. Next thing you know, you're being led farther into the backyard. To the shed.

Your grandpa opens the door and ushers you inside. You can hardly believe what you see.

Find out what's inside the shed on **page 97**

"Tomorrow night. In the woods. Bring more of this to me. Or else."

The words are part instructions, part threat. You gulp as the giant rabbit stares you down.

You feel the wet pitcher begin to slide down your shirt as Smalls lets go of it. You grab it. By the time your hands stop shaking, Smalls is already gone.

You wait a moment, then collapse in a heap on the floor. Your mind is racing.

Are you really going to bring lemonade to a monster rabbit? What choice do you really have? And what did he mean by "or else"?

You run over these questions in your head until you doze off sometime in the early morning.

*Wake up on **page 174***

PAGE 104

The sound of breaking bones echoes in your ears. The Rabbit Woman crumbles to the floor. Behind where she once stood is another figure.

The Rabbit Man! The one who tried to help you before you ran off.

As you come running over, he drops the huge rock he used to bash the Rabbit Woman in the back of the head. You're so happy you could hug him. But you don't. Not yet. You have other problems to solve first.

The Rabbit Woman lays at your feet, her body twitching.

"Is she going to be okay?" you ask.

"I don't know," the Rabbit Man says. He reaches down and removes the rabbit's foot from around her neck. He adds it to his necklace, which now has more feet than it did when you first met him. "But let's not stick around to find out. C'mon."

Follow the Rabbit Man to **page 182**

PAGE 105

You're out in the open now. In a small field of some kind. There are tufts of thick purple grass all around you. The sky above is a dull shade of red and punctuated by angry streaks of blue-white lightning. The humidity is intense, like it could start pouring down rain any second.

You pull on your shirt collar and look around. Not too far away from where you stand are some trees. They're tall, thick, and blue, but at least they have leaves and vaguely resemble the trees you're used to.

Looking in the opposite direction, you see more open fields. The fields stretch on for miles it seems.

If it is about to rain, maybe it wouldn't be a bad idea to have some cover. The trees, as strange as they are, would help with that. But walking through a forest may make it harder for you to find help. If there is any help to begin with...

Better make a decision quick.

Head for the trees by going to **page 155**

Head out towards the fields by going to **page 207**

PAGE 106

You hold your breath so you can hear everything clearly.

"Yeah, I'm still out here, over." It takes you a second, but you're able to place the voice. It's the cop who picked you up earlier. You wonder what he's still doing out here.

As if on cue, there's a pop of radio static and the cop says, "I'm still looking for that kid. Sounds like they're the grandkid of the folks who run Bunny Buddies Estates. Little shithead ran off on me, over."

There's a garbled response and another slice of static.

It's then that you realize the cop is approaching you. You don't think he's seen you, but you don't take the chance. You press yourself flat against the ground.

The cop's radio crackles again. He's standing right over you; the only thing separating you is a tree.

"No, I know. The kid won't get harmed. Don't worry. I'll find 'em, over."

Harmed? Shit, maybe there really is something dangerous going on out here. Whatever the case, you need to get out of here. If the cop is telling the truth, maybe he can help.

Or maybe it's just a trap.

Reveal yourself to the cop on **page 151**

It's a trap and you know it, so stay hidden on **page 87**

When you wake up next, you're in your room. You get up in a flash, rush down the stairs, and enter the kitchen. You find your grandparents there making lunch.

"What happened to Mr. Bundinni?" your voice cracks embarrassingly.

"Who?" your grandpa says from his seat at the table.

"Mr. Bundinni! What happened to him?"

"We don't know what you're talking about, kiddo," your grandma replies. "But here, have some lunch."

She hands you a piece of celery. But you don't want the celery, you want to know what happened to Mr. Bundinni. Is he hurt? Is he de—

You know what? Actually, you do want that celery. You take it and scarf it down. Your grandmother hands you a carrot and you wolf that down too. She alternates between sticks of celery and carrots until you're so full, you could bust. You feel content. Even a little docile.

Your grandma smiles at your grandpa. "Looks like our newest little test subject is going to work out nicely."

THE END...?

PAGE 108

The rest of the day is pretty chill. Your grandparents ask the typical questions about school (it's good) and how your parents are getting along (fine, you guess). Eventually the conversation just fades out, drowned in glasses of lemonade and old game shows on TV. The shows are a little basic, but it's kinda funny seeing your grandparents shout the answers at the TV. This would never happen back at home. You can't even remember the last time you watched TV with your parents.

The summer heat persists well after dark, and eventually your grandparents decide to call it a night. You consider staying up a bit later, but all the rabbit décor on the walls is giving you the creeps. You head up to your room and try to sleep.

As you stare up at the ceiling, you think about home. Think about your parents enjoying their summer while you're stuck here in the backwoods.

You roll onto your side and gaze out the window overlooking the bed.

And then you start to hear something. It's faint at first. Then it gets louder and louder.

You wrap your pillow around your head, hoping it'll stop, but it doesn't. It just keeps getting louder. And it's coming from outside.

Investigate on **page 95**

You feel a sharp stab in your chest. And then warmth spreading out all over your clothes. You look up and meet Lauren's face.

You try to gargle out the word "why," but it doesn't come. There's too much blood filling up your lungs. But Lauren understands. She pulls out her necklace of rabbit feet. Four of them. The last time you saw her, she only had one.

And then it clicks. *The others.*

"I want to win," she says simply. She checks you over for a rabbit's foot as you slowly bleed out.

She doesn't find one though. In her disappointment, she leaves. She's the last person you see before you die.

THE END

You tell her enough of the truth to make her believe you. You say how you saw Mr. Bundinni killing rabbits in the shed. You casually leave out that your grandparents were there or that there was a weird altar. She seems to take the case of animal cruelty seriously and sends some officers to investigate in the early morning.

She ends up calling your parents and cutting their vacation short. You go home and a few days pass before your parents sit you down and explain what happened.

Apparently, Mr. Bundinni (whose real name was Jeffrey Tinkle) had found some reviews of Bunny Buddies Estates online and decided to worm his way into the operation. You see, Tinkle had a thing for hurting animals, especially the small and cute kind. He had a criminal record in a few states but always managed to avoid any serious jail time. When he arrived at Bunny Buddies, he manipulated your grandparents into letting him stay with them. He used a cocktail of drugs to keep them confused and disoriented, which wasn't as hard as you'd think. Your dad admits that both your grandma and grandpa had been mentally slipping over the past few years, but he had no idea it was that bad.

The police found dozens of rabbits buried out in the backyard, most likely killed by Tinkle. A criminal case is currently being built against him. Your grandparents, meanwhile, are being moved into a nursing facility.

It might not have been the summer you wanted, but at least it's over.

With Smalls gone, the other rabbits scatter into the nearby woods. You don't see any hint of them staying around for the remainder of the summer.

Bunny Buddies Estates officially closes, and the remaining rabbits and cages are donated to a local animal shelter. Your grandparents just can't stand to look at those beady, little eyes after what's happened.

You spend the rest of the summer helping clear out their house of all things rabbit related. You can tell there's a bit of sadness in your grandparents' eyes, getting rid of everything that they once loved.

But there's good news too. They've decided to move to Florida. Away from all the carnage.

When your parents finally come to pick you up at the end of the summer, your grandmother offers you a cup of nitro lemonade for the road.

You're about to decline, thinking of the headrush, when she says, "It's my last batch. There won't be any more after this."

You take the cup, drink it down. "Thanks, Grandma."

Your parents honk the car horn from the driveway.

"Go on, kiddo."

You head out the door but turn back one last time. You smile at your grandparents, knowing that this story is all over.

THE END

PAGE 112

"How about you work for me and my friends? You help make the elixir and you stay alive. Or…"

Smalls slides his paw across his throat.

You swallow hard. What kind of a choice is that?

"That's what I thought," Smalls's voice breaks through into your brain. "Now, get to work."

---

*What other choice do you have? Turn to **page 16***

PAGE 113

You immediately get to work trying to chew through the cage. You try to wrap your mouth around the wire walls but can't seem to get a good hold of anything. Your mouth just isn't wide enough. Plus, it kinda hurts after a while.

Later in the day, you move on to trying to bite through the wire flooring. There, you only manage to successfully fill your mouth with some incredibly funky flavors you'd rather not think about.

"How about you try some real food?" the brown rabbit suggests with a laugh. "You know. Instead of poop and metal."

He hops over to the feeding trough next to the gray rabbit. He takes a bite of the food, looks over at you, and says, "C'mon over."

---

*Get a bite to eat on **page 56***

PAGE 114

You decide to listen to the voice and dart down the left path. You barely pass the split in the path when a shadow leaps out from the surrounding darkness. It grabs you, wraps itself around you, and pulls you off the path and into the darkened woods.

*Go to **page 72** while you still can...*

The party mostly consists of you being introduced to other members of your grandparents' rabbit cult. Well, not just your grandparents' cult anymore. It's your cult too!

Indeed, your life is gonna change now. As you meet the other members, you're reminded of your duties to praise Grandifal the Great Rabbit and of the literal sacrifices you'll be asked to make. More than one member even quips about not getting stingy with the sacrifices. But with your grandparents supplying you with the rabbits, you should totally be in the clear to live out a long and mostly happy existence (once you get past the slaughtering of innocent animals part).

Eventually you get brave enough to ask about what would happen if you didn't make any sacrifices.

"Oh, horrible, soul-tormenting things would happen to you, kiddo!" your grandmother says with a laugh. She hands you a piece of the rabbit-shaped cake someone brought.

And with that, it looks like your fate is baked right into the cake.

All hail Grandifal, right?

PAGE 116

You unpack your things, and a little while later, your grandmother calls you down for dinner. You rush downstairs expecting one of your grandma's famous feasts only to find…

"Carrots? And celery?" You look at the plate before you in utter shock and disappointment. The carrots don't even look cooked. And the thought of getting the stringy cords of celery stuck between your teeth makes you want to gag. "But where are the—"

"This is what Mr. Bundinni likes," your grandmother says. "*This* is what we *all* like."

You turn to your grandpa, hoping for some kind of support. But his eyes never leave his plate. He munches on the cold vegetables in front of him without a word.

Mr. Bundinni, meanwhile, seems enraptured with the meal. He "*mmms*" and "*ahhhs*" throughout eating his carrots and practically sucks down a stalk of celery in one go. If you weren't hungry before, you definitely aren't now.

The meal comes to an awkward end, without you eating more than a few bites of carrots.

Go to bed hungry on **page 125**

You march outside followed by your grandparents. As soon as you exit the house, a guard tries to stop you. But you're quick. Before it can even lay a paw on you, it's shrunk back down to normal size.

Suddenly, your head throbs. You clutch the side of your face. It's like someone jabbed an icepick behind your eye. In an instant, your grandma is by your side.

"Are you okay?" she asks as she gently grabs your arm.

"Yeah," you utter through the pain. "Let's just find Smalls and get this over with."

You take a step forward and the world rushes around you. Could this be a side effect of the nitro? Is this why Smalls always acted like he was in pain?

You push through the pain. You have to.

Go to **page 206**

PAGE 118

Your heart skips a beat. "My grandparents did this to you?"

"Yes," Mr. Bundinni says. "They lock me up at night. There's a key in their room though. Won't you please get it?"

"I don't know…"

"Please!" Mr. Bundinni cries out. He immediately covers his mouth, realizing he's spoken quite loudly. "Please… The key to the cuffs is in their room. Please. Hurry."

You nod your head. He seems distressed, you think to yourself. You can't just leave him chained up. You have to help him.

"I'll be right back," you say and head out into the hallway.

You cross the hall and slip inside your grandparents' room.

Look for the key on **page 181**

You manage to pull yourself up and out of the pit. Once you're out, you fall onto your stomach, thankful to be on solid ground again.

You can't believe what you've just learned. That the booby traps are real. That this *game* is real. If only you had listened to the Rabbit Man, maybe none of this would have happened. Maybe the cop would still be alive. And maybe you wouldn't be shaking as bad as you are.

You try to get up off the ground, but your arms and legs feel like Jello after climbing out of the pit. You've got to calm yourself down.

You close your eyes and try to steady your breathing. Your breaths go in and out, in and out until your racing heartbeat finally calms down.

Slowly, you open your eyes. Only a few feet away from you stands a shadow.

A shadow with tall, pointy ears.

Go to **page 63**

PAGE 120

"I want to go home," you whimper. "I want to go home. I want to go home. I want to go home!"

Your grandma touches your shoulder. "I'm sorry, kiddo. That's just not an option right now. We need to hurry, and we can't wait for your parents to show up. So, what's it going to be? Are you coming with us or staying here?"

---

*Go with your grandparents on **page 179***

*Decide to stay in the house on **page 65***

You hop up on the windowsill. You peer down the side of the house, to the ground below. It's only two stories down, but it feels much, *much* farther.

Your four furry feet become unsteady, wobbly on the narrow windowsill. You've never had to balance like this before. One of your feet gives way and slides out from under you. Then another.

A second later, you're tumbling out the window.

Falling through the air.

Hitting the ground.

Experiencing the end.

FIN

PAGE 122

You take a step back, trying to put some distance between you and the Rabbit Woman. But she's not having it. She takes a step towards you.

You take another step away, but she's right there.

You slowly slide to the left, and she follows suit. You realize then that she's mirroring your every move. She's fucking with you.

As you stare her down, that's when you see it. The glint in the moonlight.

A knife?

No, a scalpel. Clenched tightly in her fist.

The Rabbit Woman cocks her head to the right. The rabbit mask's soulless black eyes peer back at you. It's like they're asking you what's it going to be? What's your next move? How do you want to die?

Take the offensive and try to rush her. Go to **page 142**

Fuck the offense. It's time to run to **page 188**

Two can play at this game. Start mirroring her on **page 152**

PAGE 123

For whatever reason, you're pretty confident you can find a booby trap to lure the Hare into. You start walking through the woods, circling around a little bit.

Pretty soon, the Hare notices.

"Stop fucking around, kid, and get me out of here."

He holds up the cleaver and the gun. Would he really use them on you? Are you really willing to find out?

---

*Turn back and take him to your grandparents on **page 10***

*Keep going with confidence on **page 128***

PAGE 124

You're just a kid. How are you supposed to stop an eight-foot tall were-rabbit? Surely, your grandparents will know what to—

Their screams invade your ears, shattering your train of thought. You slump to the floor, unable to move. You don't know how long the screams go on, but it feels like forever.

At some point though, they do stop because you hear the monstrous Bundinni emerge from the room. He closes the door and heads down the hall toward you.

The house is dead silent until he says, "See ya, kiddo. Have a nice summer."

He disappears down the stairs and that's the last time you ever see Mr. Bundinni.

Later that night or in the morning (time is an illusion at this point), you call your parents.

You say the only thing you can think to say.

"I think you need to pick me up."

END

That night, you lie awake in your bed. You've tried to sleep but can't. Things are just so different here this summer, and you know it's all Mr. Bundinni's fault. You wish he'd just go away so things could go back to the way they were.

You turn on your side and your stomach rumbles, begging for food. A few more grumbles later, you sit up in bed. You look toward the closed bedroom door.

Surely no one would know if you went downstairs for a midnight snack, right?

But then again, you might make your grandma mad if she catches you. Maybe you'll be fine until morning. After all, you can't have carrots and celery for every meal, can you?

Go downstairs by turning to **page 7**

Try to sleep by going to **page 164**

You scan the yard for something to distract Smalls. You spot the rabbit cages near the house. If he's so concerned about the rabbits, maybe that's your best shot.

You break into a run, the cut on your stomach pulling and tearing with each hurried step.

You begin to open the cages and shove the rabbits out. They bounce around on the ground, but it's not enough to get Smalls's attention. You start stomping around them, trying to scare and scatter them even more. You chase them away from the house and toward the woods.

"Smalls!" you shout. "Look!"

He turns his attention toward you and sees the empty cages. He sees the last of the rabbits dashing into the dark woods.

"Nooooo!" he roars. "Come back!"

You see worry flash across his face. The telekinetic connection breaks, and the house drops back onto the ground with a seismic boom. Smalls races into the woods and disappears.

Turn to **page 51**

PAGE 127

"Okay..." you say with some hesitancy.

"That's a good kiddo," Mr. Bundinni says. He nods to your grandpa, who leaves the shed. A moment later, he returns carrying in another rabbit. He places it in your arms and gently pushes you toward the altar.

Mr. Bundinni picks up the knife and offers it to you.

"Are you ready, kiddo? More importantly, are you willing?"

---

*Yes. Go to **page 153***

*No. Turn back to **page 88***

Your confidence is rewarded… just not in the way you'd hoped.

Because you eventually do find a booby trap. You're just too slow to prevent yourself from falling into it. The stakes at the bottom of the pit slide right through you as if your body was warm butter.

The Hare, meanwhile, escapes totally unscathed. Maybe you should have let the adults handle the situation rather than trying to deal with it yourself.

THE END

"I saw you all drinking blood back there!" you yell. "I saw—"

Powerful footsteps march into the room. It's Mr. Bundinni. Before anyone has time to react to his sudden presence, he grabs the cop's head and jabs a knife right into his throat. Shock wells up behind the cop's eyes. His mouth parts, and blood spills out onto his shirt and the floor.

Mr. Bundinni pulls the knife out, and the cop collapses on top of the coffee table. The empty glass of nitro lemonade shatters as it hits the floor.

"Look what you made me do!!" Mr. Bundinni shouts. "Look what you made me do!!"

You think for a moment he's talking to you, but he's not. His glare is directed straight at your grandparents.

"You should have never allowed a child to come here!" he screams. "You've wrecked everything! All my work! All my rituals. All my—"

He stops. He whirls around to face you. Two mighty steps later and he's in front of you. He leans down in your face. "And you're going to pay."

Go to **page 96**

You close your eyes and flood your mind with pictures of cute, tiny, harmless rabbits. The images flip through your mind, faster and faster.

You open your eyes and see Smalls stomping across the yard toward you. You focus on him, try to envision him getting smaller.

And magically, he does! With every step, he shrinks by nearly a foot. The sneer on his face disappears. The hatred burns out of his eyes.

He becomes nothing more than a rabbit.

You drop to the ground, utterly exhausted. Your grandma wraps her arms around you as your grandpa grabs Smalls before he can hop away.

Soon, Smalls is back in his cage, as if nothing ever happened.

"I'm sure glad that nightmare is over," your grandpa says with a bit of a laugh.

"C'mon, let's go inside and have some lemonade to celebrate," your grandmother suggests.

"That's okay, I think I'll stay here a minute," you say. "I'm pretty tired of lemonade anyway."

They head inside, leaving you alone with Smalls.

"Not so tough now, huh?" you say.

Smalls stares back at you for a moment with those dark round eyes, then winks.

Every sound is enough to cause your heartbeat to spike. From the squeaks and creaks of the old house, to the occasional bug bumping into the window glass, you're definitely on edge. You desperately want your grandparents to come home.

At some point, you get up and look out the living room window. You gaze out into the darkness of the night. There's no sign of them. Or Bundinni for that matter.

You settle back down on the couch. And that's when you hear it.

A soft knocking at the front door.

Are you going to answer it?

Yes. Turn to **page 183**

No way. Turn to **page 165**

PAGE 132

One of the shadows rushes toward you and the Rabbit Man. You prepare yourself to run as the shadow wraps itself around him.

"We're so glad you're safe!" the shadow cries.

You realize that another rabbit-clad player, this one a woman, has locked the Rabbit Man in a bear hug.

"Shhhh!!" the Rabbit Man hisses back at her. "You're gonna get us caught if you keep shouting like that."

The woman lets go of the Rabbit Man, ignores his comment, and immediately turns her attention toward you.

"They let kids get involved in this?" she asks to no one in particular. "These people really are insane."

"I'm not... I'm not part of the game," you say. "Who's running this thing anyway?"

"Some real sick fucks," says one of the other players who has crossed the clearing to greet you. "And you're playing this game, whether you like it or not."

Turn to **page 198**

Before you can ask who "they" are, the rabbit creature formally known as Mr. Bundinni springs up and heads for the hallway. He rips the door off its hinges and exits the room.

You follow behind him, terrified of what's about to happen.

He stops in front of your grandparents' bedroom door. You can hear your grandparents shouting from within their room, wondering what's going on. Mr. Bundinni casts one final glare at you and enters your grandparents' room.

What do you do now?

*Try to stop him from hurting your grandparents on **page 192***

*Wait and hope for the best on **page 124***

PAGE 134

You open the cage door. Despite his large size, Smalls squeezes through the opening. He jumps out and slams into your chest with all his weight. You fall backwards onto the concrete slab.

As Smalls hops away into the summer night, you could have sworn he said something to you. But that's impossible. Rabbits can't talk.

And yet, two words hang in the air. You know you heard them.

Two simple words.

"Thank you."

Turn to **page 137**

PAGE 135

You want to scream, but the sound suffocates in your throat.

The cop's unblinking eyes are fixed on you. They're wide and unsettling. It's as if they're screaming at you to run. You take a step away from the hulking rabbit.

A grin flashes across his face. There's a fierceness to his guy. A wildness. Even his costume is more rabid, covered in mud and… blood? It's then that you notice the necklace. It's packed with rabbits' feet. Maybe half a dozen or more.

Oh god. Does that mean he…?

You remember the words of the Rabbit Man.

"Not all rabbits are the same…" The words leave your mouth without you even realizing it.

The behemoth lets out a curt laugh. "That's right. I'm a hare." He bends down by the cop's body and stands back up. He cocks his newly acquired gun. "And I just leveled up."

Fucking run to **page 37**

You gotta get out of here!

You throw your blanket up in the air and jump out of bed. The blanket floats in front of you and drifts overtop the were-rabbit's furry face. The beast suddenly starts to go nuts trying to get the blanket off. It jumps and bucks around the room. You see its back legs trying to kick the blanket off, but it's no use. The blanket is huge.

Now's your chance!

You see an opening to the door. You make a run for it and—

In its struggle to remove the blanket, the were-rabbit kicks you in the chest and sends you flying across the room. You break through the glass window and fall a story below.

When you hit the ground, it's not just the window that's broken anymore. So is every bone in your body.

On the bright side, you have a wonderful view of the stars and the moon as you bleed out.

THE END

PAGE 137

You pick yourself off the ground, dust off your pajamas, and head back inside. You give one last look to the yard, but Smalls is nowhere to be found.

Upstairs in your room, you try to sleep, but you can't get those two words out of your head. Someone said thank you. But who... *or what?*

You barely get any sleep that night. You're exhausted when your grandma calls you down for breakfast in the morning. You're about to doze off in your oatmeal when your grandpa comes bounding into the kitchen, his heavy boots thudding against the floorboards.

"Damn rabbit got loose again," he says.

"Which one this time?" your grandma asks.

"Smalls," your grandpa says. "Door was wide open!"

You stare down into your bowl of oatmeal and push the pale brown sludge around with your spoon.

"I just don't get it," he says. "How in the hell are they always getting loose?"

"They're smart critters," your grandma says.

"Yeah, yeah, yeah." Your grandpa storms out of the room. The house rattles as he slams an outside door shut.

Your grandma takes a sip of coffee and then asks the question you've been dreading. "You wouldn't happen to know how Smalls got out, would you?"

"No, not a clue," you say. You scoot your chair out from the table. "I'm gonna go back upstairs for a bit. I didn't sleep too well last night."

Before your grandma can say another word, you dart out of the kitchen.

Turn to **page 55**

PAGE 138

Without even realizing it, you're heading back toward the house and away from the shed. The image of your grandparents' faces—their open mouths—is burned into your brain.

This has to be some kind of dream, right? This can't be happening. Your grandparents wouldn't drink… the thought sickens your stomach.

But you know what you saw. In fact, you're pretty sure you'll never forget it.

You stop halfway through the yard. You decide you have two choices. Pretend that this never happened, that you never saw a thing. Or get the hell away from this freak-show as fast as you can.

What's it going to be?

Pretend nothing happened and go to **page 173**

Run away on **page 22**

PAGE 139

You decide to tell them about your grandparents, Mr. Bundinni, and the shed. The four listen with bated breath as the grizzly details pour out of you. Once you're done, Warren is the first one to say anything.

"That's messed up," he says.

"Your grandparents and this Bundinni guy must be the ones running things," Lauren says. "If it's their property and everything, they have to know what's going on."

"Think they know their own grandkid is out here, though?" Monique asks.

"They're about to," Jim says as he grabs ahold of your shoulders. "Think this kid is our ticket out of here."

*Find out what trouble telling the truth has gotten you into on **page 74***

"You see, kiddo," Mr. Bundinni continues, "rabbits are more than just symbols and representations of life, youth, and vitality. They *are* life, youth, and vitality. Contained within each and every one of them is a magic that can be harnessed. Utilized to extend life far beyond what modern science is capable of. And what's even better is they breed so fast, there's never a shortage of supply."

"You-you can't be serious," you say. You look to your grandparents, hoping for some kind of explanation, some sort of denial. Instead, their eyes flick away from yours.

Your gaze falls to the rabbit in your grandma's arms, then to the rabbits in the cages, and finally the knife resting on the table. A creeping dread starts to wash over you.

Mr. Bundinni sees the pieces coming together in your head. He smiles a yellow, toothy grin. "It's time for you to choose, kiddo. Do you want to live forever… or not?"

Accept Mr. Bundinni's offer of never-ending life on **page 127**

Decline the offer on **page 47**

You take another step away from the Hare, trying to build a little bit of distance between the two of you.

It doesn't work.

In a split second, he's closed the gap.

"Please!" you shriek. "Please, don't hurt me. I'm not even supposed to be out here. I'm-I'm not part of the game. I'm Martha and Greg's grandkid. I'm not supposed to be here!"

The Hare looms over you. Staring you down.

"Please," you beg.

"Hmm," he says. He lifts the cleaver to your throat, tilts your chin back. "You don't look like the other rabbits. And you don't have a rabbit's foot."

"Exactly! Because I'm not part of the game!" Your chest swells with hope. Maybe he's actually going to let you go!

He lowers the cleaver. "But maybe… maybe I can still use you."

Find out what you've gotten yourself into on **page 157**

PAGE 142

You gather up all your courage and charge at the Rabbit Woman. There isn't much ground to cover, so it's a quick charge and you haven't really thought about what you'd do when you got there.

But the Rabbit Woman clearly has. With effortless grace, she slashes the scalpel across your throat as you draw near and then dodges to the side.

You crash to the forest floor, soaked in your own blood. You grab your throat to staunch the bleeding and turn over onto your back. The Rabbit Woman is now standing over you. She pushes your hand away from your throat. Blood jets onto her mask. She doesn't even flinch.

"No rabbit's foot?" she says. "Fucking pointless."

She recedes into the darkness of the woods. The last thing you ever see before you bleed out.

THE END

"Yeah, I'm fine," you say. "Sorry, just a little disoriented."

"Well, let us help you get oriented," the brown rabbit says. He bends his ear to the left. "Over there you got your water, and right next to it is your food. There! You're oriented!"

"Thanks…"

"You still don't look too good, new guy," the gray one says. "Maybe you should have something to eat."

"Yeah… maybe…"

The two rabbits hop toward the feeding trough. It takes you a second to realize they're waiting for you to join them. But should you?

---

*Join them for a meal and head over to **page 56***

*Decline to eat and go to **page 93***

PAGE 144

Standing in front of the fridge is a monster. A big, hairy monster. Standing on two feet, it's guzzling down a pitcher of your grandma's lemonade.

A part of you (you can't tell if it's a courageous part or a stupid part) tells you you've got to get this monster out of the house. What if your grandparents came down here and found it? What would it do to them?

Another part of you tells you to be patient. To observe this thing. To figure out why it's drinking lemonade in your grandparents' kitchen in the middle of the night.

You think it over in your head and decide to…

Confront the creature on **page 67**

Continue watching it on **page 150**

Mr. Bundinni's foot is the first thing to touch the moonlight, and it immediately elongates and doubles in size. A thick coating of fur spreads across his sweaty skin. He lets out a moan as his body cracks, shifts, and breaks.

You pull the covers closer to your face, but you stare on in horror as Mr. Bundinni becomes more beast than man. Fur now covers his body. His back is arched. He lifts his head toward you, his gleaming, black eyes reflecting in the moonlight. You see his oversized front teeth. His tall, pointy ears.

He's a were-rabbit, and he's blocking the room's only exit!

What are you going to do?

Make a run for it on **page 136**

Accept your fate and hide under the covers on **page 5**

PAGE 146

The living room lamp comes on. You were right about the man on the couch not being your grandpa. The tall ears should have given it away that it was another rabbit-clad player.

His hand rests on the arm of the couch, a meat cleaver in his grasp. Fresh blood drips from the blade onto the floor. You follow a drop of blood down to the floor and see…

Turn to **page 196**

You race towards the woods, your legs pumping as hard as they can. You expect to hear another gunshot head your way, to rip through you, and spill your blood all over the ground. Thankfully, it never comes.

You slip through the gap between two thick trees and race deeper into the woods.

Forest darkness is different than regular nighttime darkness. It's thicker, harder to see through. Shadows loom and creeping plant life sprouts from every possible angle, trying to touch you, to snag you, to consume you. Almost immediately, you feel a low, thin tree limb tear at your face. Your bare feet are stabbed with rocks and sharp, sturdy grass.

You curse yourself for not grabbing shoes earlier.

You push farther into the woods when you suddenly stumble upon a path. It's unkempt and overgrown with weeds, but it's a path nonetheless. It forks a few feet ahead of you with one path leading to the right and the other one to the left.

You pause for a moment to consider your options. That's when you hear it.

The soft rustling sound and then the strained, whispered words, "Left! Go to the left! Hurry!"

If you listen to the voice and choose the left path, go to **page 114**

If you choose the right path, go to **page 15**

PAGE 148

Later that night, you're speedwalking through the yard carrying an extra full pitcher of lemonade. Grasshoppers and crickets jump through the night air and away from you.

You near the tree line of the surrounding woods, but you're not sure where to go from here.

"Smalls?" you call in a strained whisper. "Smalls?"

You peer into the darkness. You turn, the lemonade sloshing in the pitcher. Finally, you hear it.

"Over here."

You see Smalls's form rise out from behind a thicket. You take a step toward him, but he's already next to you.

"I'm so glad you brought it," he says. "I knew I could trust you." He snatches the pitcher from your hands, raises it to his lips, and guzzles it down.

As the last drop of lemonade disappears into the rabbit's mouth, the pitcher slips from his grip. It falls to the ground and shatters.

You dance away from the broken glass. You expect Smalls to do the same, but he's just staring upward, eyes fixated on the sky.

"Smalls? Are… are you okay?"

Slowly, he lowers his head. His gaze meets yours, but it doesn't seem like he's looking at you so much as through you. His mouth hangs open ever so slightly. After an eternity, two words escape.

"Your… family…"

Find out what he's talking about on **page 75**

PAGE 149

Your grandma takes you upstairs to show you to your room. You've never seen her with this much energy. Usually, she's pretty slow-moving and suffering from arthritis. This time, though, she took the steps two at a time! You practically have to speed walk to keep up.

When you reach your room, she stops. "Same room as always," she says with a bit of song in the words. Suddenly, her eyes narrow and her face hardens. "Mr. Bundinni will be staying in the room next door. Under no circumstances are you allowed to go into his room. You got that, kiddo?"

You nod, uncertain of why she's issuing such a stern warning. "Who is this guy anyway?"

Your grandma ignores the question. She opens your door open and says, "You're probably hungry after such a long trip. I'm going to get started on dinner. I'll call you down when it's ready."

She beams a smile at you and heads for the stairs.

You hang by your door and look at the closed door to Mr. Bundinni's room.

Who is this guy? What's in there? And why was Grandma so weird about going in there?

A voice pulls you out of your thoughts. It's your grandma's. She's standing on the stairs, the intersection of the floor and stairs making it look like she's cut in half. "Remember, kiddo. Don't. Go. In. There."

... but do go to **page 116**

PAGE 150

You hide behind the doorframe.

"I know you're there," a deep voice booms.

Your heart skips a beat. You pray that didn't just come from the creature.

"I know you're there," it says again. The creature lowers the pitcher of lemonade and turns toward you. "And I could use your help."

Your heart pounds in your ears. This… this thing is talking to you. And worst yet, it looks familiar. The brown fur. The nose. The ears.

"Smalls?"

"I've… I've been having visions," the hulking beast says. "Horrible… unspeakable visions, but this… nectar…" He lifts the pitcher, and it shines in the refrigerator light. "It provides clarity. Calmness."

The massive rabbit takes a step toward you, and you flinch in fear.

"I need more of it," Smalls says. "Please. You've helped me once. Now, help me again."

You take an uneasy step forward. "But I don't know how to make it. It's my grandma's secret recipe."

Smalls closes the gap between the two of you in an instant. He shoves the still-cold pitcher into your chest.

"THEN FIND OUT."

Turn to **page 103**

You pick yourself off the ground, careful not to make too much noise for fear of the cop overreacting. You slowly approach the cop, who's still busy talking into his radio to notice you.

"C-can... can you help me?" you ask.

The cop turns toward you, radio still near his mouth. "Found the kid. I'm bringing them in, over."

He hooks the radio back into his belt and grabs your arm. With a slight shove, he moves you forward.

"You're not going to hurt me, are you?" you ask. "I heard you say you weren't going to hurt me."

"Let's just get you back to the house," he says.

The two of you march in silence for what feels like forever. Your heart is pounding, and anxiety is coursing through your veins. He said he wouldn't hurt you on the radio, but can you really believe him?

The cop has his own questions to ask.

"Which way?"

"What?"

"Which way? Do you know which way leads back to the house?"

He points ahead of you. There's a dirt path, forking off to the left and right. You wonder if it's the same path you saw earlier.

"Well, which way?"

Definitely right. Go to **page 26**

Definitely left. Go to **page 45**

PAGE 152

You cock your head and hope the Rabbit Woman takes the bait. An agonizingly long minute passes before she moves again. She takes a step (more of a glide honestly) to the right. You mirror her.

She stops and cocks her head again. You do the same. You can tell she's thinking. Maybe this will work out for you. Maybe she'll leave you alone after all.

The Rabbit Woman takes a step forward. You step back. Another step, and you're right there. She raises her arm, lifting the scalpel into the sky. You do the same with your arm, except you're painfully aware that you don't have a weapon of any kind.

Suddenly, her body language relaxes. She knows she's got you beat because that blade will make all the difference.

She brings her arm back down, points the scalpel right at you and—

CRACK!!

Hurry to **page 104**

You grab the knife and nod.

"Good," Mr. Bundinni says. He begins speaking in a language you've never heard before.

Your ears hum. Your heart pounds. You can't believe you're doing this.

The knife slashes across the rabbit's flesh. Red blood rains down onto the floor. And the world around you goes black.

*Wake up to your new life on **page 166***

PAGE 154

You creep out into the hallway. Thankfully, there's no one out there to stop you from spying on Mr. Bundinni.

You tiptoe to his door. Your heart beats faster as the whispering gets ever so louder. It's definitely coming from his room. You can hear it through the closed door.

With a shaking hand, you reach out and pinch the doorknob with your thumb and your index finger. You twist the knob slowly and ease the door away from its frame. A slit of the room becomes visible from the doorway, and you can't believe what you see.

Turn to **page 29**

Thunder roars above you as you head for the tree line. You can't help but wonder where on Earth you are. You've never seen anything like this. It doesn't even seem like Earth.

Your stomach drops at the thought that maybe you're not on Earth at all anymore.

You pick up the pace as you near the trees. That's when you hear it.

SNAP!

You stop dead in your tracks.

Something else is here. Cloaked in the shadow of the tall trees. Whatever it is, it's big, you realize.

You take a step back, but the shadow moves toward you. And then you hear an all too familiar voice.

Go to **page 98**

PAGE 156

Your arms tense up, but they can't support your weight. Your grip slips away from the pit's edge. Bits of dirt come falling down with you.

At least it's a short trip to the end of your story.

FIN

"Use me? What do you mean?" you ask.

"You're from around here. You know this place. Better than I do anyway," the Hare says. "I want you to lead me out of here. I want to talk to the folks in charge."

"But I don't know who's in charge."

"Oh yes, you do," says the Hare coolly. "You said their names just a moment ago."

Your heart thumps in your chest. "My grandparents?"

The Hare nods. "And that prick Bundinni. You're going to take me to them. Now."

He returns the cleaver to your throat. You close your eyes and think.

You can't bring this homicidal maniac to your grandparents, can you? Even if they are running some fucked-up game, they're your grandparents. What if he hurts them? What if he ki—

But what if he hurts *you*? It's not like you signed up for any of this. You were supposed to have a nice summer with your grandparents. Now, you're in some fucked-up game with killers, booby traps, and—

Booby traps. Maybe that's your way out.

The cold metal of the cleaver tugs at your flesh, reminding you to make a decision and fast.

Take the Hare straight to your grandparents as best you can on **page 10**

Try to lure the Hare to a booby trap on **page 123**

"Let's get the hell out of here," you say with a bit of a grin.

"You heard the kid," Jim says. "Let's go."

The five of you stick close together as you make your way through the woods. You don't know if it's intentional or not, but you're in the middle of the pack. You feel safe with these people. You feel like together you all can handle anything that's thrown your way.

Well, almost anything.

A few minutes into your little excursion, you encounter another group of players. Seems everyone had the same idea about teaming up. But these folks aren't like the ones you've joined. No, these ones are armed with sharp knives and even bigger clubs. Their rabbit costumes are soaked with blood and bits of brain matter. Between the group, there's a dozen rabbit's feet.

They make short work of you and your friends. If only you'd teamed up with them instead. Oh well, nothing you can do about it now since this is the end for you!

OVER

"Don't shoot!" two voices shout at you in unison.

You point the shotgun down at the floor and breathe a sigh of relief. It's your grandparents! They look tired and sweaty, but still in one piece.

"You almost scared the crap out of me! Why were you knocking?" you say.

Your grandparents exchange quick but noticeably nervous glances.

"The door was locked, silly! Besides, we didn't want to frighten you by bursting in here," your grandma says as she pushes past you and into the house. Your grandpa follows quickly behind her. That's when you notice he's clutching his hand. You also notice that they don't have their guns anymore. That must be a good thing... right?

You follow your grandparents into the kitchen. "Did you get Bundinni?"

"Oh yes," your grandmother says, while your grandpa washes his hands in the kitchen sink. "We took care of him. Now, why don't you head on up to bed?"

She pushes you out of the room and toward the stairs. You go up a few steps but glance back just in time to notice the slash on the back of her leg. If you squint, you'd almost say it looks like a bitemark.

*Turn to **page 38***

"No." You're scared, but your voice doesn't wabble. You're proud of yourself for that at least.

You stare down Smalls as best you can. You see the rabbit's nose twitch. His eyes shift back and forth. And then, you feel the ground beneath your feet as he lowers you back down.

You sigh in relief as he turns away from you.

Then in a flash, he whips back around. You feel a stinging sensation across your abdomen. An angry warmth begins spilling out of you.

Turns out rabbits have claws, and Smalls isn't afraid to use them.

You fall to the ground, sticky with the mess of your own innards. As you watch Smalls head toward the house, you know it's all over for you.

THE END

PAGE 161

Strong, fur-covered arms pick you up by the armpits. "Time to get to work," a deep voice says.

You and your grandpa are hauled out of the cellar by two massive rabbits. You're brought inside the house and thrown onto the kitchen floor. Thankfully, your grandma is there, too, and still in one piece. She looks exhausted, her face stained with tears. She's frantically stirring a pitcher of lemonade, but she manages to look over and smile at you.

You're about to get off of the floor when a rabbit steps in front of you.

Smalls.

His head has grown in size since the last time you saw him. The back of his head has elongated, making him look like one of those weird parasitic aliens from a movie you saw a long time ago. He flashes a jagged-tooth grin at you.

"Long time, no see, *kiddo*."

He doesn't move his mouth, yet you can hear every word he's saying.

"I know we didn't get off to a great start," he continues telepathically, "but how about I make you a deal?"

Hear Smalls out on **page 112**

PAGE 162

"Need some help?"

As soon as the words leave your mouth, your grandparents freeze. They turn around to face you. Your grandma holds a squirming rabbit in her hands.

"Hey kiddo," your grandpa says. "What are you doing out so late?"

"I could ask you the same thing," you say with a bit of a laugh. "Is there a problem with the rabbits?"

"No, no… I mean, yes, yes, there is," he stammers.

"But we'll take care of it," your grandma adds quickly. "Why don't you go back to bed?"

They really don't want you out here for some reason. But why? What's going on?

Insist on staying by going to **page 102**

Go back inside like your grandma suggests on **page 169**

You and your grandpa spend the rest of the summer working for Mr. Bundinni. You cook, clean, wash dishes, and do whatever else he demands of you to avoid the same fate as your grandmother. Outside, you and your grandpa work to keep the rabbits alive and fed, until Bundinni decides it's time for another sacrifice.

On the rare occasion you get to go into town, it's to gather supplies for Bundinni's spells and rituals. You're never left alone for very long in the stores though. It always feels like someone is watching you.

It's not the type of summer job you ever expected to have, but you are learning a thing or two about magic and immortality. Maybe you'll be able to put it on your resume when you're older. That is, if you ever do get older. Mr. Bundinni has you and your grandpa on a high-magic diet. You may just end up working for him forever. Literally.

PAGE 164

You lie back down on the bed and try to get some sleep. An hour passes and you're still awake though. Your stomach continues to grumble, but now, in between your stomach's pleading, you're also hearing a strange whispering sound. It's barely noticeable at first, but the more you hear it, the more undeniable it is.

You toss off your sheets and walk around the room, careful not to make any noise. You near a wall and you're sure the whispering is coming from just the other side.

It's Mr. Bundinni's room, you realize.

What could he possibly be whispering about in the middle of the night? You just have to find out.

Go to **page 154**

PAGE 165

Nothing could make you answer that door. You rush to shut off the living room lights, grab the shotgun, and huddle up on the couch.

A second later, the knocking stops.

You strain to hear anything besides the incessant ticking of the rabbit clock.

Suddenly, a violent crash explodes from somewhere within the house. You press yourself into the couch.

You hear footsteps approaching. Big. Heavy. Footsteps.

If you could crawl inside the couch to hide, you would.

A shape cuts through the darkness of the house and settles by the entrance to the living room.

What seems like an eternity passes before you hear three little words.

"Hi there, kiddo."

What do you do?

*Fire the shotgun at the shape. Go to **page 189***

*Try to blend in with the darkness. Go to **page 76***

PAGE 166

You wake up in your bed. The sunlight pouring in through your window is blinding and forces you to squint. You sit up slightly, and your head begins to pound. You're tempted to go back to sleep when your grandmother opens your bedroom door. She comes in carrying a tray loaded with bunny-shaped pancakes and a tall glass of nitro lemonade.

"Here you go, kiddo," she says, as she lays the tray across your lap. "You had a big night last night."

Your stomach drops and you remember the rabbit. The rabbit you…

"That really happened?"

"'Fraid so, kiddo," she says. "Now, eat up. We have a big surprise for you downstairs when you're ready."

"I don't think I'm hungry…"

"Hush. Now, eat up, and we'll be downstairs whenever you're ready," your grandma says. She heads for the door but turns around before she leaves. "Just don't keep us waiting too long." She winks and heads out the door.

Well, you heard her. Don't keep them waiting. Hurry to ***page 58***

You approach the cage door. You can clearly see that it's latched shut. You try to fiddle with the clip keeping the door shut, but your paws are just too big and awkward to get at it. You try for several minutes before eventually giving up.

You should have known better. If it was that easy, any rabbit could get out.

It's time to reevaluate your options.

Try chewing through the cage on **page 113**

Try causing a ruckus on **page 71**

PAGE 168

You run toward the shed, with the cop following quickly behind. If you can get to the shed first, you think, maybe you can prove to him that something fucked up is happening.

You push your legs as fast as they can go.

And you make it to the shed.

You push the door open and rush inside. Your grandparents and Mr. Bundinni turn toward you. There's shock on all their faces, but more than that too. Blood is smeared all over their shirts and mouths. Limp and discarded rabbit corpses litter the floor.

"What in the hell?" a voice behind you booms.

It's the cop. And he's just seen with his own eyes what you'll never forget.

Go to **page 89**

"Okay. Goodnight, and good luck with the rabbits."

You head back inside and make your way to bed without another thought.

You spend the rest of your summer eating celery, carrots, and various homemade fruit and vegetable smoothies. You watch old game show reruns with your grandparents and Mr. Bundinni. But you watch something else too.

Each night, you see your grandparents go out to the backyard and grab one of the rabbits from the cages. They take that rabbit to the shed out back, but the odd thing is, they never come back with it. You'd investigate but you're a good kid who does what they're told. Who doesn't cause trouble by getting too curious.

So what if your grandparents are getting hairy patches all over their bodies? Who cares if their teeth are getting bigger or their ears are getting a little elongated? That's just part of getting older, right?

That's what you think… for a while anyways. Then one morning you come down the stairs to find two giant rabbits sitting at the kitchen table. Mr. Bundinni comes in and smiles a smile that makes your stomach feel queasy.

"Our Bunny Buddies just got a whole lot bigger," he says and hands you glass of indeterminant veggies. "But I think we have room for one more."

You down the smoothie, because why not?

PAGE 170

You lean over toward your grandpa.

"Do you think you can take the guard?" you whisper.

"Maybe. Why?"

"I just need you to hold him off. Just for a little bit."

He nods.

"On the count of 1… 2… 3!"

You rip the pitcher of lemonade out of your grandma's hands, as your grandpa whips around to grapple with the rabbit guard. You guzzle down the lemonade, a good portion of it spilling onto your shirt. It doesn't matter though. You reach for another container of lemonade and down it as best you can.

You hear your grandpa straining against the guard.

More! You need more! You drink every bit of lemonade you can find.

You turn to face the guard.

Time for the moment of truth!

Use your psychic powers on **page 186**

Downstairs in the kitchen, your grandmother pours you a glass of her famous nitro lemonade and sets it in front of you.

"You're gonna need that to stay awake," she says. "It's gonna be a long night."

"Why? What's going on? Please, just tell me!"

"You saw with your own eyes, kiddo," your grandma says as her husband comes into the room carrying two shotguns. "Bundinni is a were-rabbit."

"We were trying to help him and his condition," your grandpa says. "We were trying to find a cure. That's part of the reason we've been running Bunny Buddies Estates all these years. Your great-grandfather Jeremiah was afflicted the same way."

"And we dealt with him just like we'll deal with Bundinni," your grandmother says. "He's just too dangerous to keep alive anymore. Going after a kid like that…"

"Wh-what are you going to do?" you ask.

"Stop him. One way or another. And you're going to help."

*Go to **page 176***

PAGE 172

Together you, your grandparents, and Mr. Bundinni proceed outside. You stop briefly by the rabbit cages, where your grandmother pulls one of the rabbits out. She holds it tightly as you all head to the shed.

Your heart beats faster with every step. You don't want to go inside, not after what you've seen, but what choice do you have?

Mr. Bundinni takes his place next to the altar. You notice a knife sitting on it. Your grandma stands next to him with the rabbit.

"It's time," Mr. Bundinni says. "Eternal life can be yours, kiddo. But for a cost. Are you willing to pay it?"

*Go to **page 140***

PAGE 173

Are you crazy? You seriously think the best idea is to pretend you didn't see your grandparents and their wacko friend drinking rabbit blood? These people could be dangerous! They could be drinking more than just rabbit blood, ya know.

*So, how about this? Turn back to **page 138** and try again*

*If this is the second (or third or fourth) time you've come to this page, go to **page 25***

PAGE 174

You wake up to the sound of footsteps coming down the stairs. It takes you a second to remember where you are. You're still cradling the empty pitcher of lemonade, and it jogs your memory. Reminds you of the monster in the kitchen. To its strange demand for lemonade. To its threat.

Before your grandma enters the kitchen, you pull yourself off the floor. Your heart is pounding, but you tell yourself to act normal.

"Well, you're up early," your grandma says. "And already hitting the nitro, I see."

You force a smile as she takes the pitcher from you.

"Here, I'll make some more," she says.

She slips the pitcher under the faucet and begins to fill it with water.

Now's your chance! What are you going to do?

If you ask Grandma for her lemonade recipe, go to **page 201**

If you spill the beans about Smalls instead, go to **page 49**

PAGE 175

Your grandmother cleans up the wound as best she can, but it's still yellow and oozing when she puts a long Band-Aid over it.

"Why don't you get some rest, kiddo?" she suggests.

You head up to your room on the second floor. It's a little stuffy in there, so you open a window. Next, you plop down on the freshly made bed and peel back the bandage. It's still gross and gooey under there. Maybe the bite really is infected. You bring your hand closer to your face for a better look. The citrusy smell of lemons invades your nose. Might just be the smell of whatever antibacterial cream your grandma put on it though.

You put the Band-Aid back on. You're not even there for an hour and you've already hurt yourself. *The summer sure is off to a great start*, you think sarcastically.

You turn on your side and decide to take a nap as a way to reset the day. You close your eyes and soon drift off to sleep.

Catch some zzz's on **page 24**

PAGE 176

"I can't help!" you shout. "I don't know anything about hunting or were-rabbits or anything!"

Your grandma and grandpa look at each other.

"Maybe it's better if the kiddo stays here," your grandpa says.

"But what if Bundinni comes back here? We can't leave 'em all alone," your grandma replies. "It'll be much safer with us."

"Don't I get a say in any of this?" you chime in.

They exchange uneasy glances. "Sure, what do you want to do, kiddo?"

Ask to go home and escape from all this madness on **page 120**

Agree to go with your grandparents on **page 179**

Decide to stay in the house where it's safe on **page 65**

You're led farther into the police station. You're fingerprinted, have your picture taken, the whole nine yards. After all that's done, you're sat down in a waiting room. The beehive hairdo lady kneels down to your eye level. She offers you a cup of cocoa. You take it, but you don't drink any of it.

"You know, we're only here to help," she says.

You don't respond. You see her eyes fall to your pajamas. And then to your dirty bare feet.

"You're not a runaway, are you?" she asks. "But you were running away from something, weren't you?"

You lift your eyes from the cup of cocoa and meet hers. "*Tell me.*"

Tell her the whole truth on **page 14**

Stretch the truth on **page 110**

PAGE 178

The cop lifts you off the ground. Seeing your injured foot, he curses softly to himself. He then picks you up and starts carrying you out of the woods.

"You know, that's what you get for running off without any shoes on. Hopefully you didn't break anything."

You stay silent as he brings you back to your grandparents' house a few moments later. He sets you down by the door and rings the doorbell.

Immediately, your grandparents open the door.

"Oh, thank goodness," your grandmother shrieks. "We were so worried when we couldn't find them. Thank you! Thank you, officer!"

The cop tips his hat. "Just doing my job," he says. "Mind if I come in for a moment? Kid was heavier than I expected, and I could use something to wet my whistle."

"Oh… o-of course," your grandma says. She slides away from the door.

The cop gives you a quick wink and enters the house.

Go to **page 190**

"I'll come with you guys," you say.

"Then you're gonna need this," your grandmother says. She hands you a shotgun.

You take it. You can't help but feel awkward with it. It's long and heavy. You've never gone hunting before in your life. Maybe you should stay home where it's safe.

But before you can change your mind, your grandmother is already pushing you out the door.

The night air is thick and humid. A huge full moon hangs above you. The nearby woods are alive with chirps and cheeps from critters of all sorts.

You follow close behind your grandparents as they stalk through the yard. They're pros and you can tell. Their movements are smooth and graceful. Yours, on the other hand, are awkward and jerky.

You have a bad feeling about this as you approach the edge of the woods. You really don't want to go in there.

"Stay here, kiddo," one of your grandparents whispers. "We'll be right back."

They slip into the darkness of the woods, leaving you all alone.

Go to **page 82**

PAGE 180

"Where are you taking me?" you shout as you try to free yourself from the guards. It's useless though. They're too strong for you. The more you struggle, the tighter their grip gets on you.

They push you into another room, and Mr. Bundinni follows behind.

You lash out at the man who caused all this to happen. "You-you *bastard!* Make them let me go!"

"Now, now, kiddo," Mr. Bundinni starts, "you really shouldn't be using that kind of language. Where you're going is actually quite special. You might even get the chance to peer upon the face of Grandifal himself."

"Who the fuck is Grandifal?"

"Such blasphemy," Mr. Bundinni says, shaking his head. He produces a piece of chalk from his pocket and kneels down. He begins drawing an elaborate symbol on the floor by your feet. "You must show respect to the Great Rabbit, should you meet Him." He tucks the piece of chalk back into his pocket, his artwork complete.

He claps his hands and the artwork ignites. A swirling portal forms on the floor, and a second later, the guards push you into it.

Teleport to **page 57**

Your grandparents are sound asleep in their bed. Both of them are snoring, although your grandpa is snoring much louder. You look quickly around the room, hoping to find the key in clear sight. You check on top of a dresser and a chest of drawers, but don't find anything. But then you spot the end table by the bed. A ring of keys sits on top of it.

You sneak over, careful not to make too much noise. You pick up the keys. They jingle in the air, and suddenly, the room falls silent. Your grandparents both stop snoring. You freeze.

Are they going to wake up?

Find out on **page 53**

PAGE 182

You follow the Rabbit Man through the woods for the remainder of the night. There's a lot of stopping and listening and waiting, but at least you don't encounter any other players or booby traps.

You honestly can't believe you're still alive when you see the sun start to come up through the trees.

The two of you race toward the sun and eventually make it out of the woods and arrive back at your grandparents' house. There, you find several of the other surviving players all lined up and being inspected. The Rabbit Man joins them and to your shock, it turns out he's the player with the most rabbit feet for the night. He earns his freedom and a fat stack of cash.

As he's turning to leave, he glances over at you. He hands you a few hundred bucks and tells you to get out of here while you can.

He doesn't have to tell you twice. You head on down the road and make a break for it. With any luck, you'll be able to find a ride and be home before you know it.

Congrats! You survived the night at Bunny Buddies Estates!

THE END

You grab the shotgun and head for the front door. Your whole body trembles with each step.

The knocking continues. It's steady. Calm. Unlike you.

You gulp down a bit of your fear as you grab the cold, metal doorknob. You turn it slowly. The lock clicks open.

With that, you rip open the door and aim your shotgun at whoever—or whatever—awaits on the other side.

*Go to **page 159***

PAGE 184

"I…" you start and then stop. "I… I got… lost."

Skepticism forms over the others' faces, but they don't challenge your explanation.

"Well, now that we're together, we have some strength in numbers," Jim says. "Figure we can either hunker down here for the night or try to get out of here."

"I vote for getting the fuck out of here," Warren says.

"Me too," Monique replies.

"I don't know," Lauren says. "I think we're safer where we are."

"Think I'm right there with you," Jim adds. "So, a tie. Which means you're the tie-breaker, kid. What's it going to be? Should we stay or should we go?"

If you think the group should stay where they are, go to **page 200**

If you think they should leave, go to **page 158**

It's like a birthday party exploded in your grandparents' living room. Bright, colorful streamers hang from the ceiling. Balloons drift lazily throughout the room. A banner is spread across the mantelpiece that reads "WELCOME TO THE CULT." And there's people. Tons of people you don't recognize there. They're all wearing pointy, plastic party hats and looking at you.

"Surprise!" they shout in unison. "Welcome to the cult!"

Your head pounds from the sudden jump in noise level. You desperately want to go back upstairs, to run away from all this, when Mr. Bundinni grabs you by the arm.

"May Grandifal bless you, kiddo," he says with a yellow-toothed smile.

"What? Bless who?"

"Why, Grandifal! Our cult's patron and the supreme rabbit being!" he says. "You better hit the books and learn your cult history, kiddo."

Your grandparents appear by your side. "Oh, don't worry about that," one of them says. "There's all the time in the world now that they're immortal. Praise Grandifal!"

Go to **page 115**

PAGE 186

The guard thrashes against your grandpa, but your grandpa is able to hold his own. For now.

Think, you tell yourself. *Think!*

You focus on the rabbit guard for a moment and then close your eyes. You hold onto the mental image of the guard and then visualize it turning back into a rabbit. A small, normal, adorable rabbit. One that couldn't possibly take your family hostage and force you to make lemonade. You run the sequence through your mind over and over again.

Your grandpa lets out a brief grunt, and you open your eyes.

Your grandpa is standing in front of you. On the floor is a rabbit. A normal-sized rabbit. It hops around the kitchen like nothing happened.

You look up at your grandpa and smile.

"Let's get Smalls."

*Jump over to **page 117***

You lift the gun, point it at the approaching sound, and pull the trigger.

And nothing happens.

You pull the trigger again and again, but it doesn't do anything. You look at it puzzled, when an angry, blood-soaked Bundinni monstrosity emerges from the woods.

Maybe you should have asked how to use the gun *before* you went hunting for were-rabbits.

Just sayin'.

THE END

PAGE 188

You take off in a flash. You expect the Rabbit Woman to follow you, but when you glance back, you see her just standing there.

Yes! She's letting you go! How lucky is—

The ground beneath you gives way. Before you know it, you're falling back down into the pit you just climbed out of moments ago.

Except this time, there's no getting out.

The stakes pierce your body—your flesh—and slide right through you.

THE END

Fear takes over and you shift into autopilot. You fire the gun at the shape. The shot goes high though, blowing a hole in the entryway's woodwork, and thank goodness it does. The lights snap on, and your grandpa is standing there. His eyes are wide with sheer terror.

"Don't shoot!" he yells. "Don't shoot, kiddo!"

You set the gun down on the couch just as your grandmother comes rushing in.

They're both alive (no thanks to you, of course)!

A quick round of hugs is exchanged. Your grandparents tell you they didn't catch Bundinni. He's still out there somewhere. Your grandparents say you all will have to be ready in case he returns.

So, it looks like you'll be hunting were-rabbits for the rest of the summer.

After some target practice first though.

THE END...?

PAGE 190

Before you know it, your grandparents and the cop have settled in the living room. Your grandmother brings in a glass of her famous nitro lemonade, and the cop downs it in a single gulp.

"Mighty fine lemonade, ma'am," the officer says. He sets the glass down on the coffee table. He clears his throat and continues. "Now, the kid here said they saw something going on in the shed out back. Something about... animal sacrifices? That sound familiar to any of you?"

Your grandparents look confused. They shake their heads. "No, no... not at all, officer."

The cop's eyes narrow. "Any reason for the kid to lie?"

Your grandpa smiles wide and innocently. "Always did have a big imagination, that one. Isn't that right, kiddo?"

"Yeah," your grandma says. "Tell the officer it was just your imagination."

The cop looks at you. What's it going to be? The truth or a convenient lie?

Tell the truth about what you saw in the shed on **page 129**

Admit to lying about what you saw in the shed on **page 195**

You make a beeline for the hallway. Once there, you close Mr. Bundinni's door and head toward your grandparents' room. Whatever is going on, they'll explain it.

You push open the door to their bedroom and shake them awake. You tell them confusing fragments of what's going on. About how Mr. Bundinni is shackled in his room. They get up and escort you out of their room. They usher you down the hall, past Mr. Bundinni's door, and into your room.

"It's okay, kiddo," your grandma says as she closes the door behind her. "Just get some sleep."

But sleep is the last thing you can think about at a time like this.

You sneak up to your door and put your ear to it. You hear your grandparents arguing in hushed tones out in the hallway. About "throwing away years of research" and "were-rabbit test subjects." About how "Bundinni's too dangerous to keep any longer." You want to go out there when you hear footsteps move away from the door. A moment later, there's more footsteps heading into Mr. Bundinni's room. The door squeaks. You hear a click. And then the deafening boom of a gunshot.

*Go to **page 70***

PAGE 192

You realize you have to act fast. You need some kind of weapon. You look down at the shattered remains of Mr. Bundinni's door and grab a chunk of it. You race into your grandparents' room.

The were-rabbit Bundinni looms over your grandparents, who are still in bed, cowering and afraid.

You charge at Bundinni and jab the splintered piece of wood into his back.

He roars and swats you away. You crash into a tall chest of drawers. The heavy chest wobbles back and forth before it starts to tip over on top of you. And then…

SPLAT!

THE END

PAGE 193

The five of you enter your grandparents' house. The doors are unlocked, which isn't surprising all the way out here, and the house is dark, which also isn't surprising since it's the middle of the night. But there's an air... a feeling in the house. A feeling that something isn't quite right.

"Grandma? Grandpa?" you squeak.

Jim immediately puts his hand over your mouth. "I'll do the talking."

You enter the living room. You kick something at your feet, and it rolls across the floor. It stops next to the couch... where someone is sitting.

Jim pushes in front of you. "We have your grandkid, old man," he says. "Give us the prize money and you can have 'em back."

The man stays perfectly still, and in that moment, something dawns on you. You tug on the back of Jim's costume.

"That's not my grandpa."

Turn to **page 146**

PAGE 194

"I'm free," he says.

In a flash, Mr. Bundinni is up off the floor. He paces the room, stretching his arms, his legs, his muscles. With each loop around the room, you notice he's... changing.

He's getting bigger. Stronger. Hairier.

"Mr. Bundinni..." you say. "What's going on?"

"I'm free," he repeats. "I'm finally free from their magic shackles. I'm—"

He suddenly falls to the floor. You hear flesh ripping and bones cracking, breaking, shifting. Mr. Bundinni writhes in agony as his body transforms into...

A monstrous rabbit creature. Tall, furry ears now stand on top of his head. His yellow teeth are large and sharp. And his eyes... The candlelight dances inside his dark, round eyes.

"I'm freee-aaaaghhgh," Mr. Bundinni moans. "And now, they dieeeeee."

*Quick! Head to **page 133***

You drop your shoulders. "I was… lying."

You know that's the true lie, but you've already caused too much trouble tonight. Better just to end this now before you make it worse.

The cop looks at you. Disappointment is written all over his face. But maybe somewhere deep down, a little bit of relief too. "Kinda figured that was the case. I won't take up any more of your time then. Goodnight."

Your grandparents escort the officer out the door. They watch him leave and only when they're sure he's gone does Mr. Bundinni emerge from the other room. He puts a hand on your shoulder.

"You did good, kiddo. And now, we have something to show you."

Find out what on **page 172**

PAGE 196

Your grandfather's severed head. The one you accidentally kicked across the room.

You gasp and you think you hear the others do the same.

"Oh that?" the other player says. "Yeah, I took care of him just before you got here. The old lady and the other guy too."

The other player—your grandparents' murderer—stands up. He looms large in the crowded living room with his ears practically touching the ceiling.

"Thought they might be worth some points or something," he continues. "But I was wrong. And I hate being wrong."

In a flash, he crosses the living room. With break-neck speed, he slaughters the other players one by one, leaving you for last. You try to leave, but you just end up scrambling over dead and dying bodies. The other player picks you up, lifts you into the air, and stabs you just as—

*Go to **page 199***

The next few days play out in agonizing slow-motion.

Late on the first day, the police arrive just as the sun sets. Their blue and red lights flash repeatedly across the yard.

You catch snippets of the officers talking as they search for you. Words like "disappeared" and "without a trace" and "runaway" slip from their lips.

They search all over the property for hours but find nothing. But you already knew there was nothing for them to find. You're not lost after all. You're right there. Just… trapped and… different.

You don't see your grandparents for days. By then, the food pellets have all run out. Not that you were going to eat them anyway, but the other two rabbits… they're hungry. And angry. They know you did this to them. Caused them to be neglected. To them, you're a harbinger of doom. They're a superstitious lot, these rabbits, and they won't go down without a fight.

One night (you're not sure which one), you wake to them kicking, biting, and scratching you. You put up a bit of resistance at first, but your energy quickly gets zapped away. It all seems so pointless. You're never going back to how things were.

They rip and tear into your flesh—out of hunger or desperation or anger, you don't know. But you do know one thing. This… this is…

THE END

PAGE 198

You all quickly exchange names. The Rabbit Man is Jim. The woman who was so eager to see him is named Lauren. Then there's Warren and another player named Monique. They also tell you how they were drugged and brought out here to play out some person-hunting experience. They found each other by chance and decided to pull their resources in order to survive the night. But then the conversation turns towards you.

"Why are you here, kid?" Jim asks. "How did you get mixed up in this?"

You think about what led you to running into the woods in the middle of the night. You think back to the shed and your grandparents killing those rabbits. You look around at the players, each wearing a rabbit costume. This can't be a coincidence, can it? You have a bad feeling you know who the "sick fucks" running this game are.

Your chest aches with indecision. Should you tell them or pretend not to know anything? Is it safe to trust them?

Tell them about your grandparents on **page 139**

Hide the truth from them on **page 184**

You sit up in your bed. Drenched in sweat. You pat yourself down looking for cuts and stab wounds, but there aren't any. It was just a bad dream!

You breathe a sigh of relief and fall back onto the bed. You're still in your grandparents' house, you realize, but that beats the hell out of what was happening in your dream.

After all that commotion, you know you can handle just about anything Bunny Buddies Estates might throw at you this summer.

Well, hopefully.

THE END

PAGE 200

"I think we should stay," you say. "It seems... safe here."

"Then we should set up a watch," Jim commands more than he suggests. "Cover all our vantage points."

The group spreads out across the small clearing. You pick a spot under a tree and manage to keep one of the others in your line of sight.

For the first time that night, you feel safe. So safe, in fact, you begin to nod off. It's been an incredibly long night and just a few moments' rest won't hurt... will it?

Wake up on **page 205**

You ask your grandma for the recipe. She chuckles to herself.

"Oh, a little bit of this, and a little bit of that."

You prod her some more.

"Why do you want to know all of a sudden?" she asks.

"It's for… a science project," you say, thinking quickly on your feet.

"A science project?"

"Yeah, for when I get back home."

"Well… if it's for science…" She gestures toward the fridge. "On top of the fridge are all my recipe cards. It's in there."

You hug her. "Thanks, Grandma!"

She smiles and leaves the room.

Whip up a batch of lemonade and take it to Smalls on **page 148**

PAGE 202

You're not sure how deep the cut is, but you have to help your grandparents. You don't know what Smalls has in mind, but it can't be good.

You move as fast as the laceration on your stomach will allow. As you approach the house, you feel the ground begin to shake beneath your feet. Fissures form in the ground, and they lead right back to Smalls. He's standing in the yard, arms outstretched, and eyes focused on the house. You creep toward him, still holding your bleeding stomach. You can see the veins beneath the fur on his head pulsing. Pounding. Throbbing.

You're just about to say something to him when you're cut off by an ear-splitting screech, like metal grinding against metal.

You look toward the house to see it's struggling to break free of its foundation, trying to get up into the air. But how? Did your grandma's lemonade give him more than just visions? Did it give him telekinesis?

"Smalls, stop! You can't do this! My grandparents!"

"I won't let them hurt any of us anymore," he says.

"Us?" you whisper. You realize he must mean the other rabbits.

You suddenly hear more screeching. More breaking of wood and concrete. You see the entire house lifting higher off the ground.

You have to do something and fast!

Try to reason with Smalls on **page 40**

Try to distract Smalls on **page 126**

PAGE 203

The group of you begin to move through the woods in an attempt to find a way out. You're tempted to try to run off, but Jim keeps a close eye on you the whole time.

The night drags on for what feels like forever. Your bare feet hurt, and you want so badly to sit down and rest. But that's not an option right now. And it may never be again.

You curse your parents for ever making you stay here. You curse your grandparents for getting you tangled up in this mess. And you curse Mr. Bundinni. You know this is really all his fault. If you ever saw him again, you'd...

"Look!" one of your rabbit-clad hostage takers suddenly says.

You look up and see none other than your grandparents' house.

Maybe you will have the chance to see Mr. Bundinni after all.

Go to **page 193**

PAGE 204

You shake the wire frame as your grandmother walks back to the house.

You've got to get out of here. You look all around the cage, eyes darting this way and that, but there's no way out.

"Newbie, huh?"

The voice comes from behind you. You slowly turn to see you're not alone in the cage.

Two other rabbits sit nestled in the far corner. One of them is brown and the other is gray with little patches of white.

"Wh-what?" you squeak.

The brown rabbit takes a small step forward. "It'll be okay, newbie. Those folks are a little weird, but they treat us good. You'll be fine."

Your eyes grow a little wider. Your heart thumps faster in your chest. Are you really hearing a rabbit speak?

The gray rabbit hops toward you. "You okay, newbie?"

Your mind races. You need to say something, but what?

---

*Tell the rabbits the truth and turn to **page 8***

*Play along and turn to **page 143***

The rustling of a nearby bush snaps you awake. It takes you a second to remember where you are, but once you do, you're alert as hell. Your heart starts pounding, terrified of what could be in the bush. You look around and find that the other players are nowhere to be seen.

What are you going to do when you come face-to-face with—

A squirrel?

The cute, furry, little critter scurries past you, completely oblivious to your presence.

You breathe a sigh of relief.

But then you hear more rustling. Something much bigger than a squirrel is approaching you and fast. Before you even have time to think, it lunges out and—

*Go to **page 109***

PAGE 206

It doesn't take you long to find Smalls. He's out in the backyard, barking orders at the other mutant rabbits. He has quite the army at his disposal. It's no wonder it takes him a moment to see you all standing there.

"Well, well, well," he says. "Look who's here."

"It's over, Smalls!" you shout.

You turn your head toward the other rabbits who have started to gather around him. You nod and poof! One of them is normal again. You shift your vision to the right and another one transforms. You try to take a subtle breath. A drum pounds inside your skull.

"I see you have figured out the power of the lemonade," Smalls says with a smirk. "No matter."

He narrows his eyes at you, and the final showdown begins.

---

*Go to **page 33***

You head farther out into the fields. You don't see anything but tufts of purple grass for miles. Despite the barrenness of the land, you get this odd feeling you're being watched.

The hairs on the back of your neck stand on end as you pass by a matted thicket of grass. The grass looks old and worn, like it's been dead for some time. The more you look at it, the more it looks like it's pulsing. Moving ever so softly. Like it's breathing.

You take a step toward it.

And then they emerge from beneath the grass. Two massive mutant rabbits with teeth the size of your head. They leap out from their den and are on top of you in seconds. One lets out an ear-splitting roar while the other one sinks its teeth into your neck. You scream until the blood fills your throat.

With your dying breath, you curse Bundinni for sending you here.

THE END

NAVIGATING NIGHTMARES
CHOICE CHAMPION CHALLENGE

With more than 25 endings to choose from, can you make your way through *Hare-Raising Summer* to find the endings listed below?

Checklist

- [ ] Survive the night at Bunny Buddies Estates (and earn some cash)

- [ ] Stop Smalls once and for all

- [ ] Join the Grandifal Cult

- [ ] Go hunting for were-rabbits... and live

- [ ] Reunite with your grandmother after she is sent away

HAVE YOU READ THEM ALL YET?

STAY TUNED FOR THE NEXT INSTALLMENT OF
NAVIGATING NIGHTMARES
BRAINDRAIN!

You find yourself on a mysterious stage. The lights… the cameras… They are all set and pointed directly at you. Are you ready to play *BrainDrain*?

Every question you answer on this strange trivia show has the potential to lead you closer to a million dollars… or possibly to your own demise.

So, how far will your brainpower carry you?

Can you win *BrainDrain*?

Can you afford not to?

About the Author

A.C. Bauer has been a writer as long as he can remember, and his love of the horror genre runs deep. He grew up on classic 90s slashers like *Scream* and *I Know What You Did Last Summer* and read a ton of *Goosebumps* books. He is also the founder and editor-in-chief of Cat Eye Press.

You can learn more about him at: austinbauerwrites.wixsite.com/acbauer.

www.ingramcontent.com/pod-product-compliance
Lightning Source LLC
LaVergne TN
LVHW041929070526
838199LV00051BA/2753